CREATURES OF ANOTHER AGE

CREATURES OF ANOTHER AGE

Classic Visions of Prehistoric Monsters

Edited and with an introduction by
RICHARD FALLON

VALANCOURT BOOKS

Creatures of Another Age
First Valancourt Books edition 2021

Introduction, notes and compilation © 2021 by Richard Fallon

Published by Valancourt Books, Richmond, Virginia
http://www.valancourtbooks.com

All rights reserved. The use of any part of this publication reproduced, transmitted in any form or by any means, electronic, mechanical, photocopying, recording, or otherwise, or stored in a retrieval system, without prior written consent of the publisher, constitutes an infringement of the copyright law.

ISBN 978-1-948405-74-4 (*trade paperback*)
ISBN 978-1-948405-87-4 (*trade hardcover*)
Also available as an e-book.

Cover by Xungarro   instagram.com/xungarro
Set in Dante MT

CONTENTS

Introduction

It is 1838. An incomparably strange field of enquiry has captivated the scientific world. You have heard tantalizing, disconnected scraps about it here and there for well over a decade now. Monsters alive before the age of Adam ... A former world wracked by catastrophes ... You wish to learn more. On your lap lies a volume of Gideon Mantell's sumptuous and comprehensive new book, *The Wonders of Geology*. Opening the leaves, you peer down into the sheer depths of geological time. Uncanny seas stretch before you, populated by huge crustaceans and armor-plated fish. Squinting, you gaze beyond, through sweltering jungles and lustrous lagoons, where the ill-defined shapes of monstrous reptiles loll and contort in the purple twilight. This, the author declares, is "a country more marvellous than any that even romance or poetry has ventured" to depict.[1] Absorbed in these lost worlds, you almost feel as if you were there, amongst Dr. Mantell's ammonites, iguanodons, and pterodactyls, all gone forever from the earth.

Geology and paleontology challenged scientific researchers and wider nineteenth-century publics to undergo unprecedented feats of imagination. Speculative visions of the prehistoric past, so common to us nowadays, were born of painstaking deductions, judicious analogies, and sublime moments of inspiration. Even authors writing in the ostensibly staid *Transactions of the Geological Society of London*, first printed in 1811, could not

1 Gideon Mantell, *The Wonders of Geology*, 2 vols (London: Relfe and Fletcher, 1838), 31.

always resist bursting into effusions about their outlandish subject matter, and writers targeting larger audiences were under no compunction to restrain their scientific awe. *Creatures of Another Age: Classic Visions of Prehistoric Monsters* is an exhibition of some of the variety of forms that writing about long-extinct animals took between the 1830s, when the popularity of geology and paleontology skyrocketed, up the end of the First World War, when cinema began to offer its own primordial prospects. The authors included within these pages, most of whom wrote in Britain or North America, took geoscientific research to original and creative places: necromantic fantasies, time-travel narratives, political poetry, weird *fin-de-siècle* short stories, and even pseudo-Elizabethan verse drama.

Paleontology and Geology in the Long Nineteenth Century

Although they enjoyed a long prehistory, what we now call the "earth sciences" began to take a recognizable form during the late eighteenth century and at the beginning of the nineteenth. This was a time before our solid modern notions of scientific disciplinarity and professionalization had crystallized, and as such the twin births of paleontology and geology were a heterogeneous enterprise. Nonetheless, through the work of diverse researchers across Europe and the Americas, fundamental concepts like the formerly organic nature of fossils, the distorted but chronological order of geological strata, the extinction of species, and the almost unimaginable age of the earth, took hold.[1] In this undertaking, one name rose to the top at the end of the eighteenth century: that of Georges Cuvier. Cuvier, an eminent French naturalist, examined many of the mysterious fossils that had come to the attention

1 For a concise and lucid summary by the leading historian of these subjects, see Martin J. S. Rudwick, *Earth's Deep History: How It Was Discovered and Why It Matters* (Chicago: University of Chicago Press, 2014).

of the scientific world, including the bones of a giant South American ground sloth and two types of unusual elephant, and concluded that these animals were not simply living in some undiscovered region, as might have been supposed. He declared, persuasively, that they were entirely extinct. These animals were the *Megatherium*, mastodon, and mammoth (and here it is worth noting, as the texts in this collection will soon make clear, that nineteenth-century authors were extremely erratic in the capitalization, italicization, and sometimes even spelling of extinct animals' scientific names).

The fossil remains that were uncovered from then on, or that had been sitting in the collections of perplexed learned institutions for decades, began to come under the newly scrupulous eye of Cuvier and his fellow comparative anatomists. In the initial decades of the nineteenth century a canon emerged of strange animals whose convoluted names and forms would become surprisingly familiar to the public. Their bones were spectacularly reassembled, sometimes in bravura illustrations, and at other times physically, in natural history museums. These animals included a giant deer dubbed the "Irish Elk," a similarly oversized New Zealand bird known as *Dinornis* (or moa), the famous flying pterodactyl, the aquatic reptiles *Ichthyosaurus* and *Plesiosaurus* (excavated by the working-class fossilist Mary Anning at Lyme Regis), and a group of ponderous lizards—*Iguanodon*, *Megalosaurus*, and *Hylæosaurus*—sometimes grouped under the then-obscure technical term "dinosaurs," coined by anatomist Richard Owen in 1842. Through a project substantially expedited by the Western powers' imperial rapacity, local strata and fossils were correlated and cross-referenced all across the globe, allowing researchers to piece together the chronological story of the planet's history. Most geologists agreed that this was a story of triumphant progress from the earliest primitive forms through to the complex mammals and the peak of creation, humanity.

While researchers and the public at large were gratified by the general upward thrust they saw in life's history on earth, explanations for this directionality differed. Typically, it was conceived in the light of Christianity: God had successively and mysteriously introduced and destroyed waves of animals in a divine plan that prophetically paved the way for human civilization. These ideas were eloquently formulated time and time again, perhaps most influentially in the Oxford don William Buckland's *Geology and Mineralogy Considered with Reference to Natural Theology* (1836) and the works of the Scottish geologist-journalist Hugh Miller, such as *The Testimony of the Rocks* (1857).[1] The alternative to this divine plan seemed disturbing. Complex theories of what we now call "evolution" had already been put forward, most notably by another French *savant,* Jean-Baptiste Lamarck, at the beginning of the nineteenth century. Evolution was extremely controversial, especially in the conservative societies of Britain and North America, although it was far from unpopular in certain quarters. The idea that animals were the product of biological evolution would only become something like a consensus in the elite scientific world over the two decades following the publication of Charles Darwin's *On the Origin of Species* (1859).[2] Long after Darwin, the exact causes and mechanisms of evolution were disputed, leaving plenty of room for theological and ideological maneuver.

The United States had always been a site of paleontological investigation, but it was towards the end of the nineteenth century, in the era of evolution, that it became a leading scientific power. Westward expansion into Native American lands, along with the final closure of the frontier in 1890, practically

1 For a useful text in the vast literature on nineteenth-century Christianity and geoscience, see J. M. I. Klaver, *Geology and Religious Sentiment: The Effect of Geological Discoveries on English Society and Literature* (Leiden: Brill, 1997).
2 An extensive account can be found in Peter J. Bowler, *Life's Splendid Drama: Evolutionary Biology and the Reconstruction of Life's Ancestry 1860-1940* (Chicago: University of Chicago Press, 1996).

ring-fenced some of the most impressively fossiliferous regions in the world for investigation by rich East Coast universities and mushrooming natural history museums.[1] It was chiefly in western states like Wyoming and Colorado that many of the most famous dinosaurs were unearthed between the 1870s and the 1900s: *Diplodocus, Brontosaurus, Triceratops, Stegosaurus, Tyrannosaurus*, and so on. Thanks to funding by philanthropic tycoons, their colossal bones were shipped back and displayed in opulent exhibitions.[2] By the early decades of the twentieth century, both in the United States and back in the Old World, geology and paleontology had become firmly established and considerably professionalized scientific disciplines, and no self-respecting city museum would dare open its doors without a bizarre fossil titan in its galleries.

Writing the Prehistoric Past

The scientific reconstruction of ancient landscapes and extinct animals demanded, and generated, its own literary language. This language was not simply an encyclopedia of technical Latin and Greek coinages. It also contained an array of metaphors, similes, and devices used to envision and understand an almost totally alien world.[3] Often, the new language of geology and paleontology was made from repurposed materials. Extinct animals were compared, for example, to twisted

[1] For Native Americans and paleontology, see Adrienne Mayor, *Fossil Legends of the First Americans* (Princeton, N.J.: Princeton University Press, 2005).
[2] For the motives of museum-funding tycoons, see Lukas Rieppel, *Assembling the Dinosaur: Fossil Hunters, Tycoons, and the Making of a Spectacle* (Cambridge, Mass.: Harvard University Press, 2019).
[3] For important studies to which this account is indebted, see Ralph O'Connor, *The Earth on Show: Fossils and the Poetics of Popular Science, 1802-1856* (Chicago: University of Chicago Press, 2007); Virginia Zimmerman, *Excavating Victorians* (Albany: State University of New York Press, 2008); and Adelene Buckland, *Novel Science: Fiction and the Invention of Nineteenth-Century Geology* (Chicago: University of Chicago Press, 2013).

distortions of modern species, to the chimeras of Greek myth, biblical leviathans and behemoths, the "antediluvian" creatures drowned in Noah's Flood, the dragons of fairy tales, Miltonic demons, and the intricate inventions of modern engineers. Looking back in time was like visiting a panorama or a diorama, immersive attractions that allowed leisure seekers to view large paintings and models of foreign and ancient locales. Indeed, in the nineteenth-century imagination, the pre-human world seemed to be in a state of endless volcanic convulsion, like a diorama of the perpetually stricken Pompeii. Visions of this tumultuous former world inspired the pens of famous authors including Benjamin Disraeli, Honoré de Balzac, Charles Dickens, Margaret Oliphant, Herman Melville, Walt Whitman, George Eliot, Henry James, Edith Nesbit, and Arthur Machen.

Even in the early days, romantic poets recognized the sublime scope of geology and paleontology. In his verse drama *Prometheus Unbound* (1820), Percy Bysshe Shelley conjures up

> The anatomies of unknown winged things,
> And fishes which were isles of living scale,
> And serpents, bony chains, twisted around
> The iron crags, or within heaps of dust
> To which the tortuous strength of their last pangs
> Had crushed the iron crags; and over these
> The jagged alligator, and the might
> Of earth-convulsing behemoth, which once
> Were monarch beasts, and on the slimy shores,
> And weed-overgrown continents of earth,
> Increased and multiplied like summer worms
> On an abandoned corpse, till the blue globe
> Wrapt deluge round it like a cloke, and they
> Yelled, gasped, and were abolished; or some God,
> Whose throne was in a comet, past, and cried,
> Be not! And like my words they were no more.[1]

1 Percy Bysshe Shelley, *Prometheus Unbound: A Lyrical Drama in Four Acts with Other Poems* (London: C. and J. Ollier, 1820), 138.

Scientific writers commonly inserted purloined poetic quotations like these for flights of imagination they dared not put into words themselves. Sometimes, as in the case of Edward Hitchcock and (much later) Theodore Dru Alison Cockerell, whose verses are reproduced in this collection, they wrote their own paleontological poems. Most of the earliest prose attempts to pen striking views into the world of mammoths and mastodons were written by experts like the aforementioned Cuvier, Mantell, Buckland, and Miller. Brief glimpses at first, these imaginative passages brought immense suggestive power to (often sparsely illustrated) scientific works. For instance, Mantell suggested in *Illustrations of the Geology of Sussex* (1827) that "our description will possess more of the character of a romance, than of a legitimate deduction from established facts." This false modesty disposed of, he proceeded to transport readers before the "gigantic *Megalosaurus*, and yet more gigantic *Iguanodon*, to whom the groves of palms and arborescent ferns would be mere beds of reeds," creatures "of such prodigious magnitude, that the existing animal creation presents us with no fit objects of comparison."[1]

Passages like these grew in length in the following decades, giving way to more overtly fictional forms.[2] For example, Henry Morley's "Phantom Ship" article in this volume is ostensibly a work of scientific nonfiction, but it takes the form of a fictional voyage through what we now call "deep time." George Sand's "Fairy Dust," too, is an educational work, but one of wonderful narrative suggestion and complexity. The influence of instructive nonfiction is apparent even in the most famous novel about paleontology, Jules Verne's *Journey to the Center of the Earth* (1864), in which a story of

[1] Gideon Mantell, *Illustrations of the Geology of Sussex* (London: Lupton Relfe, 1827), 83.
[2] For a history of prehistoric animals in fiction, focusing on dinosaurs, see Allen A. Debus, *Dinosaurs in Fantastic Fiction: A Thematic Survey* (Jefferson, N.C.: McFarland, 2006).

scientific fantasy is constantly balanced with detailed scientific fact.

Towards the end of the nineteenth century, part of a wave of "weird" fiction, a genre emerged in which prehistoric animals break out of their chronological chains and terrify the inhabitants of the present. Of all the stories in this genre, many of which are included here, perhaps none is more grotesque than Wardon Allan Curtis's "The Monster of Lake LaMetrie." Pitting humans against the "monsters" from deep time, these stories chillingly upset the evolutionary hierarchies that had only recently (and unevenly) begun to replace divine ones. Indeed, the somewhat lurid subtitle of this collection, *Classic Visions of Prehistoric Monsters*, in part echoes the language of the nineteenth and early twentieth centuries. Although authors of all persuasions constantly assured their readers of the reality of the peculiar animals they were describing, few could resist calling them "monsters." Seeming hodgepodges of disparate body parts, possibly even evolutionary malformations, it could be hard to sympathize with defunct animals like the dinosaurs. Nonetheless, as shall be seen in the subtle stories by Jack London and Clotilde Graves, some authors questioned where true monstrosity lay.

The most frequently quoted lines on extinct animals came from Alfred Tennyson's long elegy *In Memoriam* (1850). Here, in a moment of profound doubt, the speaker bleakly wonders if humans in a godforsaken world of "Nature, red in tooth and claw" are no better than those

> Dragons of the prime,
> That tare each other in their slime[1]

Victorians' love of dropping these memorable lines notwith-

1 [Alfred, Lord Tennyson], *In Memoriam* (London: Edward Moxon, 1850), 80-81.

standing, extinct animals could equally inspire hope, humor, and satire. Amanda Theodosia Jones's "From Saurian to Seraph" answers Tennyson's query, employing the dragons of the prime as a metaphor for the fallen state that can be bettered by Christian acts. May Kendall's jaunty "Ballad of the Ichthyosaurus" is far less pious, juxtaposing that unintellectual aquatic lizard with the modern British education system. The socialist and feminist Charlotte Perkins Gilman, meanwhile, draws upon the precedents of evolution to repudiate the arguments of those who see "human nature" as fixed, all while delivering some impressive rhymes (including one with "Loxolophodon"). Notably, these texts were written by women, who were formally excluded from many of the most prestigious endeavors of paleontological science, although women often edited or illustrated their husbands' and fathers' scientific works.[1] Constance Naden, however, was among the earliest generation of British women to receive a systematic scientific education at university level, as demonstrated here by her daringly irreverent article "Geological Epochs."

Today, we usually see dinosaurs, and other extinct animals too, through the lens of *Jurassic Park*, whether the novel (1990) or more likely the CGI-enhanced film (1993) and its sequels. The last items reproduced in this collection were originally published just as cinematic technology presented a modern way of bringing extinct animals to life, stop motion, which would be trialed in American movies like *The Ghost of Slumber Mountain* (1918) before being perfected in *The Lost World* (1925) and *King Kong* (1933). When reading this collection, it helps to look back to a dim, misty age before all these film productions: the nineteenth century, that is to say, and the dawn of the twentieth. Hopefully, like a curious reader devouring Gideon Mantell's *Wonders of Geology* in 1838, you will see the distant past in a strange new light.

RICHARD FALLON

May 2020

RICHARD FALLON received his Ph.D. on dinosaurs and nineteenth-century transatlantic culture from the University of Leicester in 2019. He is currently a Leverhulme Trust Early Career Fellow at the University of Birmingham, and his writing on paleontology and literature has been published in the *Journal of Literature and Science*, in *English Literature in Transition, 1880–1920*, and on *The Conversation*.

Edward Hitchcock

The Sandstone Bird

EDWARD HITCHCOCK (1793-1864), a geologist and theologian of Amherst College, Massachusetts, won fame in the nineteenth century for his work on the so-called bird footprints of the Connecticut Valley. These large and mysterious fossilized footprints were immensely evocative, seeming to capture delicate traces of otherwise entirely lost animals. In "The Sandstone Bird," a sorceress resembling the biblical Witch of Endor resurrects one of these huge creatures before the eyes of a geologist. Hitchcock, whose arresting interpretation of the prints was disputed, published the poem pseudonymously in the New York literary Knickerbocker *in December 1836. Its blend of humor and sublimity reflects the self-deprecation with which paleontologists often tempered their flights of imaginative speculation. Moreover, in a manner not uncommon in nineteenth-century poetry, Hitchcock offers factual footnotes to clarify the scientific content of his poem. Many decades later, the fossil footprints in question were identified as having been made by dinosaurs.*

'MAKE tracks!' reader, or in other words, stand out of the way, and let 'POETASTER' illustrate the *Ornithichnites*, or huge stony bird-tracks, of Professor HITCHCOCK, said to have been found on the red-sandstone of the Connecticut Valley. 'On reading the account of these,' says our correspondent, 'published in the twenty-ninth volume of the *American Journal of Science*, it occurred to me that there was at least probability enough in the theory advanced in that work, to make it lawful to use it in verse; and as there came up in my imagination the bird that formed the enormous *Ornithichnites Giganteus*, perhaps fifteen or twenty feet high, and with a foot seventeen inches in length, my long dormant muse was aroused to action; and before I was aware of it, I was astride of my Pegasus; and although, from original malformation or long disuse,

> —— 'he scrambled up and down
> On disproportioned legs, like kangaroo,'

yet he did not pause till he had finished his flight.' The reader shall have a glance at his paces.

The writer supposes a geologist, *solus*, examining traces of the *Ornithichnites Giganteus* on the sandstone, whose shade he apostrophizes thus:

> A THOUSAND pyramids have moulder'd down,
> Since on this rock thy foot-print was impress'd;
> Yet here it stands unalter'd: though since then
> Earth's crust has been upheav'd, and fractur'd oft:
> And deluge after deluge o'er her driven,
> Has swept organic life from off her face.
> Bird of a former world!—would that thy form
> Might reappear in these thy former haunts!
> O for a sorceress nigh, to call thee up
> From thy deep sandstone-grave, as erst of old
> She broke the prophet's slumbers! But her arts
> She may not practice in this age of light.

> ENTER SORCERESS.

> 'Let the light of science shine!
> I will show that power is mine.
> Skeptic, cease my art to mock,
> When the dead starts from the rock.

Bird of sandstone era, wake!
From thy deep, dark prison, break!
Spread thy wings upon our air—
Show thy huge, strong talons here:
Let them print the muddy shore,
As they did in days of yore.
Præadamic bird, whose sway
Rul'd creation in thy day,
Come, obedient to my word:
Stand before creation's lord.'

The sorceress vanish'd; but the earth around,
As when an earthquake swells her bosom, rock'd;
And stifled groans, with sounds ne'er heard before,
Broke on the startled ear. The placid stream
Began to heave and dash its billows on the shore;
Till soon, as when Balæna spouts the deep,
The waters suddenly leap'd toward the sky;
And up flew swiftly, what a sawyer seem'd,
But prov'd a bird's neck, with a frightful beak.
A huge-shaped body follow'd; stilted high,
As if two mainmasts propp'd it up. The bird
Of sandstone fame was truly come again;
And shaking his enormous plumes and wings,
And rolling his broad eye around, amaz'd,
He gave a yell so loud and savage too—
Though to *Iguanodons* and kindred tribes,
Music it might have seem'd—on human ear
It grated harshly, like the quivering roar
That rushes wildly through the mountain gorge,
When storms beat heavily on its brow. Anon,
On wings like mainsails, flapping on the air,
The feather'd giant sought the shore, where stood,
Confounded, he who called the sorceress' aid.

Awhile, surveying all, the monster paus'd;
The mountain, valley, plain—the woods, the fields,
The quiet stream, the village on its banks,
Each beast and bird. Next the geologist
Was scann'd, and scann'd again, with piercing glance.
Then arching up his neck, as if in scorn,
His bitter, taunting plaint he thus began:

'Creation's lord!' The magic of those words
My iron slumbers broke: for in my day
I stood acknowledg'd as creation's head;[1]
In stature and in mind surpassing all:
But now—O strange degeneracy!—one,
Scarce six feet high, is styled creation's lord!
If such the lord, what must the servants be!
Oh how unlike Iguanodon, next me
In dignity, yet moving at my nod.
Then *Mega*, *Plesi*, *Hylæ*, *Saurian* tribes,
Rank'd next along the grand descending scale:
Testudo next: below, the *Nautilus*,
The curious *Ammonite*, and kindred forms;
All giants to these puny races here,
Scarce seen, except by *Ichthyasaurian* eye.[2]
Gone, too, the noble palms, the lofty ferns,

1 Before the discovery of these Ornithichnites, the most perfect animals that had been found, as low down in the rocks as the new red-sandstone, were a few reptiles, called Saurians: so that birds must have been decidedly the most perfect animals that then existed: though it has been recently announced in the journals, that the tracks of quadrumanous animals have been found on new red-sandstone in Germany. But until I have seen the details of this discovery, I am not disposed to let it spoil my poetry: for as to some quadrumanous animals, I think that birds might successfully compete with them for the palm of superiority. [Author's note.]
2 The Ichthyasaurus, another huge and extinct Saurian animal, was remarkable for the size of its eye; the orbit in some specimens measuring ten inches in length, and seven in breadth. [Author's note.]

The *Calamite, Stigmaria, Voltzia*—all:[1]
And O, what dwarfs, unworthy of a name,
(Iguanodon could scarce find here a meal,)
Grow o'er their graves! Here, too, where ocean roll'd,
Where coral groves the bright green waters grac'd,
Which glorious monsters made their frolic haunts;
Where the long sea-weed strew'd its oozy bed,
And fish, of splendid forms and hues, rang'd free,
A shallow brook, (where only creatures live,
Which in my day were *Sauroscopic* called,)
Scarce visible, now creeps along the waste.
And ah! this chilling wind!—a contrast sad
To those soft, balmy airs, from fragrant groves,
Which fann'd the never-varying summer once.
E'en he who now is call'd creation's lord,
(I call him rather nature's blasted slave,)
Must smother in these structures, dwellings call'd,
(Creation's noble palace was *my* home,)
Or these inclement skies would cut him off.
The sun himself shines but with glimmering light—
And all proclaims the world well nigh worn out:
Her vital warmth departing, and her tribes
Organic, all degenerate, puny, soon
In nature's icy grave to sink for aye.[2]
Sure 't is a place for punishment design'd;

1 The organic remains found in the rocks of the temperate and frigid zones
correspond more nearly to those now found alive in the torrid zone, than to
those in the temperate and frigid zones. Indeed, there can be no doubt but the
northern hemisphere was once covered with tropical forests: such as the palm
and the ferns of huge size. The Calamite, Stigmaria, and Voltzia, are names
given to plants found in the new red-sandstone, which do not correspond to
any now found upon the globe. [Author's note.]
2 If it be admitted that the climate, vegetation, and animals of this valley
were tropical, when this bird lived, who will say that its present condition
would not seem, even to a rational being, in similar circumstances, to be one
of deterioration and approaching ruin? [Author's note.]

And not the beauteous, happy spot I lov'd;
These creatures here seem discontented, sad;
They hate each other, and they hate the world:
O who would live in such a dismal spot?
I freeze, I starve, I die!—with joy I sink
To my sweet slumbers with the noble dead.'

Strangely and suddenly the monster sunk.
Earth oped and closed her jaws—and all was still.
The vex'd geologist now call'd aloud—
Reach'd forth his hand to seize the sinking form—
But empty air alone he grasp'd. Chagrined,
That he could solve no geologic doubts,
Nor learn the history of sandstone days,
He pour'd out bitter words 'gainst sorcery's arts:
Forgetting that the lesson taught his pride
Was better than new knowledge of lost worlds.

Hannah Flagg Gould

The Mastodon

Throughout the nineteenth century, the mastodon, an ancestor of the elephant, was one of the most iconic prehistoric animals. Known from remarkably complete specimens, this imposing creature was often appropriated as a symbol of the raw and untamed potential of the United States. HANNAH FLAGG GOULD (1789-1865) *here addresses the mastodon in its timeless dignity. Gould was a prolific and successful Massachusetts poet and this romantic poem was first published in the July 1847 issue of the* Union Magazine of Literature and Art. *The text reproduced here is a lightly revised one from her collected* New Poems (1850). *Much like Hitchcock in "The Sandstone Bird," Gould indicates in a footnote the scientific veracity that underlay and inspired her verse.*

THOU ponderous truth, from thy long night's sleep
    Through the unrecorded eras
Awaked, and come from their darkness deep
    To this day of light chimeras!—
What wast thou, when thy mountain form
    Stood forth in vital glory?
O, who can paint thee live and warm,
    Or reveal thy life's strange story?

Those flinty darts[1] must have brought thee low,
    That were found beneath thee lying!

---

1 Several stone darts are said to have been found under the Mastodon recently discovered and exhibited. 1845. [Author's note.]

Some mighty hunter had twanged the bow,
　　Till he saw Behemoth dying!
Thou, till then, that in pride and power
　　Hadst walked the earth with thunder,
How great the pang,—the fall,—the hour,—
　　When thy life-string snapped asunder!

The ground, that, shuddering, drank thy blood,
　　In its clods dared not imbed thee;
And sea and skies gave a whelming flood,
　　As a pall, to overspread thee.
Age on age, with their stone and mould,
　　In strata deep, then made thee
A shroud no power could e'er unfold,
　　Till a day of *steam* betrayed thee.

They came,—they found, and they probed thy bed;
　　And *Resurgam* o'er thee writing,—
An ancient of the unnumbered dead
　　For too long repose indicting!—
Thee they brought to the sun's broad blaze,
　　For this rude court to try thee:—
Of high and low must thou stand the gaze;
　　And the veriest gnat may eye thee!

For rightful claim, which the world now grudge,
　　To one's own reserved quietus,
Thou com'st arraigned to each self-made judge,
　　With thine ironed limbs, to meet us.
Yet, hold on; and thy history still
　　Let none that pry discover;—
Not though they cast thee in their great mill,
　　And they grind and mould thee over!

Sublimely wrapt in a mystery be,
   As a problem grand propounded;—
The thousands prove, who may question thee,
   In their wisdom all confounded.
Heed not thou what the babblers say,—
   Be proudly mute to sages:
They're creatures all of but yesterday,
   And thou of the untold ages!

Thomas Lovell Beddoes

A Subterranean City *and* Stanzas (From the Ivory Gate)

The English author THOMAS LOVELL BEDDOES (1803–1849) *shared his time between poetry, radical politics, and medical studies. The latter pursuit was undertaken principally at German institutions, including the University of Göttingen, where he studied comparative anatomy under the influential naturalist Johann Friedrich Blumenbach. Indebted to works by Elizabethan and Jacobean dramatists, Beddoes's poetry is often weird, haunting, and macabre. Little of it was published during his lifetime. Probably homosexual, Beddoes constantly chafed against the limitations of society and became severely depressed, committing suicide in 1849. Like most of Beddoes's poems, the following two texts were first published posthumously, in 1851, by the author's friend Thomas Forbes Kelsall. Both poems, or rather fragments of poems intended for inclusion in larger incomplete works, are mysterious visions in which the deep past strangely encroaches upon the present.*

A SUBTERRANEAN CITY.

I FOLLOWED once a fleet and mighty serpent
Into a cavern in a mountain's side;
And, wading many lakes, descending gulphs,
At least I reached the ruins of a city,
Built not like ours but of another world,

As if the aged earth had loved in youth
The mightiest city of a perished planet,
And kept the image of it in her heart,
So dream-like, shadowy, and spectral was it.
Nought seemed alive there, and the bony dead
Were of another world the skeletons.
The mammoth, ribbed like to an arched cathedral,
Lay there, and ruins of great creatures else
More like a shipwrecked fleet, too vast they seemed
For all the life that is to animate:
And vegetable rocks, tall sculptured palms,
Pines grown, not hewn, in stone; and giant ferns,
Whose earthquake-shaken leaves bore graves for nests.

STANZAS.

(FROM THE IVORY GATE.)

THE mighty thought of an old world
Fans, like a dragon's wing unfurled,
    The surface of my yearnings deep;
And solemn shadows then awake,
Like the fish-lizard in the lake,
    Troubling a planet's morning sleep.

My waking is a Titan's dream,
Where a strange sun, long set, doth beam
    Through Montezuma's cypress bough:
Through the fern wilderness forlorn
Glisten the giant harts' great horn,
    And serpents vast with helmed brow.

The measureless from caverns rise
With steps of earthquake, thunderous cries,
　　And graze upon the lofty wood;
The palmy grove, through which doth gleam
Such antediluvian ocean's stream,
　　Haunts shadowy my domestic mood.

Henry Morley

Our Phantom Ship on an Antediluvian Cruise

Before authors of fiction began to introduce devices of time travel and lost worlds, popularizers of science developed innovative ways of making prehistory feel present. In this article in Charles Dickens's weekly Household Words, *journalist and educationalist* HENRY MORLEY *(1822-1894) sails his readers out of London and backwards in time through the known geological periods. The "Antediluvian" of the title figuratively refers to the time before Noah's Flood (also known as "the Deluge"). Morley's "Phantom Ship" series typically took informative trips around the world, but, as the article begins by observing, the sophistication of new leisure attractions seemed to call for bolder literary alternatives. In particular, the allusions to Leicester Square in London, and later "Mr. Wyld's Globe," refer to the gigantic hollow globe opened to the public in that entertainment district in June 1851. Morley's imaginative voyage, published anonymously two months after Wyld's Globe opened, facilitates its own three-dimensional survey of the planet through deep time.*

Now that we can visit any portion of the globe by taking a cab or an omnibus to Leicester Square, who wants a Phantom Ship to travel in? The world, as it is, has taken a house in London, and receives visitors daily. Nothing remains now for the Phantom, but a sail into the world, as it was, or as it will be. What if we steer into the future? there our vessel will assuredly be wrecked: but we desire not to be wrecked; no, since we are retiring, let us retire decently, recede into the past with a becoming dignity. For a voyage into the past, therefore, we hoist our Phantom flag: we mean to sail quite out of human recollection, to the confines of existence, and remain in dock among the Graptolites.

So we walk down Cheapside, bustle aboard at London Bridge, and sail out, leaving man behind us. Leaving man behind us; for a thousand years roll back upon themselves with every syllable we utter; years, by millions and millions, will return about us, and restore their dead before our ghostly voyage back into the past is ended. We have passed the Nore; man is behind us; man is not created: we are on the ocean of a world which has not felt the footstep of its master. Land ho! then let us go ashore. This is some part of South America; there rolls a mighty river, like the rivers that now roll over that continent; we plunge into dense forests; let us now sit down under the trees, and speculate upon that world, into which we spirits of the future have receded. There is a fallen trunk before us, on which ants and other insects swarm; there is abundance of dead vegetation under the dense shade of these living boughs. A huge creature, a colossal armadillo, looking like a tortoise very little smaller than a horse, mounted on massive bony feet, scratches and digs busily by our side, eating his vegetable dinner. He is the Glyptodon. Now, what comes? Trees fall, and underwood gives way like grass before a mighty fellow—elephant or hippopotamus? His hind legs are three times more massive than an elephant's; and look at his tremendous tail! He is not twice your height, I think, and I should guess him to be twenty feet long. We must get out of his way; he is making for this tree under which we sit. Now, with a ten-navvy-power, he is digging at the mossy slope we have deserted. He will not hurt us: his neck is short, his head is slender, and his teeth are grinders all of them; he eats no flesh, but that glorious old tree he has chosen for the first course of his dinner. Now, he has scratched a pit around it, and plants himself upon his massive hind legs, making a third supporter of his tail; then lifting his huge bulk, he throws his forelegs high upon the tree, so rocks and wrestles with it. Let us escape from its neighbourhood, lest we be overwhelmed by it in its fall. The firmest roots cannot resist so terrible a wrestler, and the great tree falls; luckily sideways. Now and then it falls upon the head of its destroyer (whose name is Megalotherium) and cracks his skull. But the skull of the Megalotherium is made thick and spongy, so that such blows crack only the outer plate, and are but rarely fatal. Now the green twigs are vanishing; the monster dines.

Aboard our ship again; as we pass out of the wood we encounter Monsieur the Mylodon, also at work upon a tree; he is not so bulky as our other friend. There is a fellow with a stiff long neck, neither a camel nor a hippopotamus, the Macrauchenia. What have we got at home? On our way home, why should we not sail round by the land, where there was New Zealand in '51? There, in the forests, run birds without wings; one, the Dinornis, greatly larger than the largest ostrich. Now, then, homeward! Ah! but where is home? "England, with all thy faults, I love thee still!" but I can't find thee, oh, my native land! Some of it is under water, some is dry land, connected with a continent not to be found on Mr. Wyld's Globe. We run up against an iceberg, floating as icebergs now float, down from the North Pole. It is aground on a raised part of the sea-bottom, and, melting there under the warmer water, is depositing the mud and gravel, and the lumps of rock or boulders that it has scraped up in its travels. When that sea-bottom shall be lifted up and become land, there will be what they call a local pleistocene deposit, and granite cropped from rocks in Norway may lie in lumps upon the soil of England. These bergs have floated down on ocean currents setting from the colder to the warmer seas.

What of the climate then? Why, as we travel back into the

past, we shall find the earth's climate in a given place, varying within pretty wide limits. Elevation of one part and depression of another part of the earth's surface is now going on, has always gone on, and probably always will go on. What is now continent has been sea before, as well as continent before, and will be sea as well as continent again. A hundred thousand years ago, Mr. Wyld, had he and Leicester Square existed, would have had to construct a model of the earth with very different coast outlines from those which now so accurately paint the land that is. But the climate depends very much indeed upon the relative position of land and sea, and the elevation of the land at given places. When, in the course of the incessant shiftings, it may happen that there is much land, and high land about the equator, and the bulk of water is at the two poles, then the temperature of the whole earth would of necessity be high. When it may happen that the land prevails about the poles, and at the equator there is chiefly water, then the temperature would be low, and ice would hold the world under its thumb far beyond the limits of the Arctic and Antarctic circles. Variations of temperature, therefore, on the surface of the earth, may, and most likely do, depend upon the physical geography of the earth's surface, not upon any special cause of heat in the interior, or upon any strange condition of surrounding air. The physical geography of the world in past ages, as a whole, cannot be ascertained. Let us suppose a geologic Wyld, who should construct a model of the earth, whereupon he arranged, with elaborate care, each under each, the modelled strata, twisted, where they are twisted, broken where broken, continuous where continuous, so that the earth's anatomy could be studied, as one can study the anatomy of man upon a *papier maché* model. From such a work it would be easy to make out, so far as it goes, contemporary sea and land through all past ages; but what shall tell us where was sea, and where was land, over almost three-fourths of the whole surface, over the part now overflowed by water? The arrangement of strata and the fossils of the submarine earth are a blank, except to our reason and imagination; of the existing dry land we have scratched only here and there upon the surface; and if we knew all, it would be scanty knowledge. It is impossible, therefore, to reconstruct the seas and continents of former ages with enough completeness for a demonstration of their influence upon climate. Moreover, when we are denied the power of examining so large a part of the earth's crust, while we may reason fairly upon what we find, and consider what we see to be a fact, we have need to be very cautious about denials based on what we have not found: most unexpected things turn up; that fact is geological as well as social. We came back to look for England, and here, not far from the Cheapside of '51, a river broad and rapid, draining a large continent, flows into a shallow sea. We sail up that river, and we call ourselves at home; though it be not our island home, the site is English. There is a monkey grinning at us. Well, we have seen monkeys in Regent Street. But there's a sort of boa-constrictor. And look through the trees, there is a tiger coming down to the river-side to drink—bigger than any Bengal tiger in the Regent's Park of '51. Let us land upon our native soil. There is an elephant, a very hairy fellow, and the Mastodon too. There's a great bison-ox, the aurochs; probably he lived long, and made acquaintance with the ancient Britons. Yonder stands gazing down upon us from the hill a mighty elk, shedding yearly a pair of antlers that weigh more than sixty pounds. The span of his horns must be a dozen feet. There is a bear; and there goes a hyæna snarling, with an old bone in his mouth, which he is taking to his kennel up in yonder cave. Any dead meat is good to him, and a fine collection of bones of contemporaneous animals, gnawed and broken, he is laying up in his establishment for the geologists of '51. There are plenty of insects buzzing in the wood; and, look, there is a vulture dipping down into the dead flesh of an opossum. There's

another serpent; and here we disturb a family of monkeys, who
pelt down cocoa-nuts upon us. There's a wolf;—a fox;—let
us go out to sea again. There is a crocodile; a turtle. There's a
bird something like a pelican. There is a strange fellow on the
shore with a long nose or a short proboscis, an odd compound
between horse, pig and elephant: what may he be? O, he's the
Palæotherium! That graceful fellow, the most graceful of all
the pig-tribe (which in this age takes the place of ruminants),
looks not unlike the thing I never nursed, a dear gazelle. 'Tis
the Xiphodon. Now we are at sea; but wait awhile before you
begin fishing, though doubtless we may catch odd-looking
things; they will be not very much unlike perch, mackerel, or
cod, or herrings. You will find no salmon. I wonder how the
salmon comes by so much patronage in '51; he's quite a *novus
homo*. To be sure, so is the best man, with the longest pedigree.
How far may we now be from Cheapside? Certainly some million of years. We have just retreated through what geologists
call their tertiary period, and fallen back into the secondary.

Shall we have to fight our way through a convulsion? No,
never fear! The three great periods are indeed separated by
breaks in the chain of the geologist: they are not, however,
breaks in nature, but in human knowledge. We have seen volcanoes on our voyage back into the past, and there is a volcano
now; but the vast effects produced by force on the world's crust
are not often produced in an instant by a grand catastrophe;
they are the results of constant force applied through enormous
periods of time. During the break between the secondary and
tertiary periods, there takes place a change in the whole series
of animals existing on the earth.

Here are sponges, and you may find the water clouded with
minute animalcules. These little microscopic fellows, whose
dried skeletons are carried by the wind like dust sometimes,
and fall on our ship's rigging—these little fellows increase and
multiply, very literally to replenish the earth. What would Mr.

Malthus have preached to the father who produces eight hundred million of grandchildren, and so on, in a single month?
Their skeletons, when they are dead, bestrew the bed of the
ocean in some places, in a layer of immense depth, part of
which, raised hereafter, will become the chalk cliffs of Old
England. When alive, these little fathers of families live on the
minute organic fragments which are about to decompose, and
become part of the dead world, but, arrested on its threshold,
make the life of these small creatures, on which larger creatures
feed and grow. There is a bird above us, like an albatross; but
if we land now, we find but few birds, no mammals, and not
very many reptiles. There is a thigh-bone some four feet long.
It belongs to a great reptile, the Polyptychodon. There you
perceive a turtle. There are some kinds of lizard; others, too,
of which we shall see larger numbers presently. Now we are at
sea again, with sharks about us. If you dredge about, you will
find star-fishes, and terebratulas, and other things that we will
look at when there's nothing else to engage our attention. Now
we pursue our phantom voyage farther back into the depths of
time—millions of years back into the past. Here is a huge reptile
like a whale that darts through the sea to seize another monster
with the claws that arm its webbed feet. This marine gentleman
is the Cetiosaurus. We land in a warm, moist country, covered
with a strange vegetation, in which fern-like palms, or palm-
like ferns, Cycadeæ, predominate. We have seen vegetation not
unlike this when we were among men in New Zealand. There
are plenty of ferns, and pines, with a few palms. Here is a land
reptile, before which we take the liberty of running. His teeth
look too decidedly carnivorous. A sort of crocodile, thirty
feet long, with a big body, mounted on high thick legs, is not
likely to be friendly with our legs and bodies. Megalosaurus is
his name, and, doubtless, greedy is his nature. Mercy upon us!
There's a young crocodile flying; look at his long jaw and sharp
teeth; he is sweeping down upon us, stretching his long neck

out. He touches ground, not after us, but yonder little kangaroo, no bigger than a rat. But now the fast little crocodile tucks
his wings under his arms—they work on an enormously long
little finger—he tucks his wings under his arms, and begins running on four legs, as if he really were a little crocodile, and not a
bird. Megalosaurus spies him; Megalosaurus is after him; away
he runs into a lake of water, swimming there like a fish; and
now lands, takes flight, and perches on a tree. Marvellous little
crocodile! bird, beast, and fish, as to its powers; reptile alone
by nature; he's the Pterodactyl, a strong, massive creature, but,
luckily, though large, he is not a giant. For a giant, there's your
reptile, the Iguanodon, with bones about eight times stronger
than an alligator's bones, thirty feet long, and half as tall again
as the tallest elephants. Don't fear. You are not a vegetable; he
will not eat you. All manner of crocodilian monsters we stum-
ble over as we make haste back to the ship.

Now we are afloat, look there, at that black, muddy-looking
lump of skin, with an immense eye in it; nothing but that
huge eye and a breathing hole above the surface. The socket
of that eye is a yard and a half round. Now, look under the
water; there's a jaw and set of teeth!—a jaw, sir, six feet long.
Twenty feet, or so, behind his glaring eye, you see where his
tail works as he shoots along. The Phantom only can keep pace
with him. There's no defensive armour on a reptile like that;
he is the monarch and devourer of whatever he surveys in the
way of meat; and what an eye for a surveyor! He is an awful
gentleman to meet when he is looking for a dinner, that same
Herr Ichthyosaurus. Sharks there are plenty of; but what are
sharks? Sharks are mere sprats to us, among these reptile monsters. If you please, we will get up that creature with a pretty
shell which looks extremely like a nautilus; it is an ammonite.
You may haul, too, for little fishes, and find sundry molluscs,
bivalves and univalves. Lo! you have caught also a great fellow
of a cuttle-fish, who has something to squirt out of his ink-bag.

An antediluvian cuttle-fish: no animals are of the exact kind
we left behind us in the days when we dwelt among men. The
skeleton in its tail it leaves as a legacy to geologists, by whom it
is received under the name of belemnite.

Farther back we go into the depths of time, and pick up
beautiful stone-lilies, animals on stems looking like lily-cups,
and having thirty thousand bits of stone jointed within a single
skeleton. There are some fish, but fewer reptiles now. The
shores look desolate. On yonder strip of sand run a few lizard-
like reptiles, one with a turtle's beak, and one with tusks. Rhy-
chosaurus and Dicynodon they are called. But yonder walks a
novelty; a frog as large as a rhinoceros; a frog as to its large hind
legs, and its mouth; otherwise very much a crocodile. There
he goes towards the water, and some birds alight upon the sand
to dress their feathers. The birds fly off; the huge frog plunges
in; and after millions of years the footmarks they make now,
with the ripples of the tide and the impression of the shower
that is now falling on the soft sand, shall be presented to the
eyes of men. The birds shall be believed in by the footmarks
they have made, though not a bone of them exist: the reptile
shall be called a Cheirotherium, because his footmarks oddly
simulate the impression of a great human hand; his huge bulk
shall perish into oblivion, but that strip of sand across which he
has walked shall tell his story for him.

We approach a black shore, and sail under the smoke and
ashes of a huge volcano; on rounding a point of rock we see
another. By this time we have travelled back through the whole
secondary period, and are about the pass into the remotest ages
of the antediluvian world. Rocks, tracts of country, hundreds
of yards thick, have, under the influence of subterranean
forces, been crumpled together like a cloth in a child's hand.
But this was the work of force and time; and over time we pass,
not caring for the breaks in human knowledge, till we find our
way back quite into another epoch.

The sea is turbulent; often we see it beaten into surf, and roaring over banks, exposed and dismal at low water. But we pass on, centuries rolling by, and sail again over the site of England. Here we find many islands, small and large; the sea is open northward to the Arctic circle. Thick forests clothe these islands, dark forests, with no bright green in their foliage. The tree ferns raise above the lower shrubs their graceful crests; the lofty Lepidodendron spreads its feathery fronds; there rises the fluted column of the Sigillaria; there are the pine-like Araucarias; and one gigantic fellow, that looks like the Norfolk Island pine, rises a hundred feet above his fellows. Ferns choke up the paths below. The paths! there is no beast or reptile living now to tread them; a few scarce birds or insects may be flitting through the scene, whose silence only winds and waves now interrupt. Rivers upon these islets float some fallen vegetation down into the sea; it is a vegetation, not of dense wood, but of plants rapidly growing, succulent or hollow in their stems. The remains of one such stem, called Calamite, resemble the jointed "horse-tail," or Equisetum, of our marshes, on a grander scale, the stem being a foot often in diameter. Another kind of stem is here, called Sigillaria, from the neat pattern which covers it; this belongs to a tree whose matted fibrous roots are called stigmaria. These, as fossils, shall belong to coal. Even in that age of the world, that '51, from which we are escaping, those who walk in tropical island forests tread upon a mass of fallen vegetation often ten feet deep. These islands, with the changes of level constantly occurring, shall sink under the wave; the sea shall cover them with sand and mud; but after a time they shall rise again, again wear the dark plumage, relieved only by the bright green of the low marshy places, again sink; and hereafter each, pressed down under the accumulated deposit of those ages through which we have been receding, shall be mined for in England as a coal deposit. Among the fossils in the coal, there will be found, chemically altered, whole trees upright as they grew—the base of a coal-field sometimes will be formed as the base of the forest is formed by the branching roots, Stigmaria, matted together. Upright stems, snapped asunder by the storm or by decay, shall be found standing as they now stand, and containing in their hollow cores the cones that drop from over-hanging trees.

We sail away, by coral reefs, and dredge for shells of mol-luscs, which we find abundant: these are reptilian fishes. That great fellow, just under our bow, with wide jaws and some teeth nearly a span long, is the Megalichthys. There are repre-sentatives also of the shark family, which, you perceive, is very ancient, or, in other words, respectable.

Farther we sail back now across the depths of time; there is no animal upon the land, and in the sea there are the shell-fish still, and many larger fishes. Agassiz, who lived in the world with us when we were dwellers among men, divided fish into four natural orders, two of them prevalent, two insignificant. Now, in this period through which we travel, those two orders, the Ganoid and Placoid, insignificant among men, prevail, and rule the ocean. There is the Cephalaspis, compared by Hugh Miller to a saddler's cutting-knife; some people ignorant of saddlers' cutting-knives might need to be told that such an instrument is like a Cephalaspis. There is the Pterichthys for which Mr. Miller found a similitude in "a man rudely drawn, the head cut off by the shoulders, the arms spread at full length in the attitude of swimming, the body rather long than other-wise, and narrowing from the chest downwards, one of the legs cut away at the hip-joint, and the other, as if to preserve the balance, placed directly under the centre of the figure, which it seems to support." This graphic account of a creature a few inches or a foot long, is much as if one compared a penny-piece to a man's head, shaved, and without features, flattened down excessively by pressure. Nevertheless, Mr. Miller—once a stone-cutter, but now a doughty Scottish editor—wrote, for

the instruction of men, a very delightful book upon that age
of the world through which we are here sailing, the period of
"Old Red Sandstone."

We have passed it now, and there are no more fishes. In a
sea broken by coral reefs swim shoals of Trilobites, wood-lousy
little fellows, with large compound eyes. The earth is desolate,
but the sun shines, the wind murmurs, and the shower falls;
the eyes used by an insect now, were needed in those days by
the Trilobite. Encrinites, too, there are enclosed in many little
stony plates, and growing on a slender stem of jointed stone.
Molluscs there are; some of them cephalopods; that is to say, of
the most developed form. These cephalopods, then, of a kind
less formidable than the cuttle-fish, were in those distant ages
monarchs of creation, the most powerful of living animals. For
we have now found our way to the confines of life.

We have reached now the Graptolites, so men name Coral-
lines, the skeletons on which lived little polyp colonies, whose
records are the first records of terrestrial life; the polyp family
being the most ancient. If we go farther now, we pass, perhaps,
the bounds of life, and we pass, certainly, the bounds of knowledge. So we run our Phantom Ship on a primeval coral reef,
and leave it there. Let it dwell with the past.

We now take to the Phantom's boats, row briskly back
through a few dozen centuries up to modern times; that is to
say, geologically speaking, to the Deluge: then, taking good
heart, and nerving ourselves for a long pull, and a strong pull,
we row gallantly into '51, and to within sight of Saint Paul's.

Charles Jacobs Peterson
(writing as Harry Danforth)

The Last Dragon

"The Last Dragon," published in the Philadelphia-based Peterson's
Magazine, *is an early precursor of the stories about surviving prehistoric monsters that would become much more prevalent in the 1890s.
"Harry Danforth" appears to be a pseudonym for the magazine's editor,*
CHARLES JACOBS PETERSON (1819-1887), *dubbed by one scholar "the
quintessential middlebrow" author of the period and a former colleague of
Edgar Allan Poe.[1] Although* Peterson's Magazine *was chiefly aimed
at women, usually publishing carefully gendered content to match, "The
Last Dragon," appearing in the October 1871 issue, is a violent adventure story set across the masculinist worlds of the gentleman's club and the
imperial frontier.*

"DID any of you fellows ever see a dragon? A real, live dragon?"

The speaker was Charley Stone. The place was the smoking-room of the Club.

"A dragon!" It was a chorus of derisive voices that replied.

"Yes! You laugh because you have never seen one. I don't
want to be rude," said Charley, coolly looking around the
circle, "but it seems to me you're quite as absurd, in spite of
your boasted civilization, as the Bengalees, who, because they
have never seen ice, think you're chaffing them, when you say
that rivers freeze over."

1 Barrie Hayne, "Standing on Neutral Ground: Charles Jacobs Peterson of
Peterson's," *Pennsylvania Magazine of History and Biography*, 93 (1969), 510-526 (512).

"But a dragon," cried Jack Stanton, with a guffaw, "a real, live dragon!"

"Yes! a dragon," retorted Charley. "Haven't we authority for it in both sacred and profane history? The Scriptures speak of dragons. The army of Regulus, in Africa, killed something very like a dragon. The traditions of all peoples and races speak of dragons, from the polished Greek to the pig-eyed Chinese."

"Myths, my dear fellow, myths," said Jack, sententiously. "There never were dragons."

"Pardon me. What else was the Saurian? Go into a geological museum, and you will see, any day, the skeleton of the monster. That settles the question, as to whether there ever were dragons or not."

"Very well put," said Jack, lighting a fresh segar. "I give that part up."

"The next point is, were they contemporary with man? Now we know that the reindeer of France, the urus, and the Siberian mammoth, once supposed to have been Pre-Adamite, survived until the human species appeared on earth. Which is the more probable, that some of the Saurian tribe lived down to the advent of man, or that the idea of so strange and abnormal a monster should have been evolved out of what the Germans call 'the inner consciousness' of a savage or savages?"

"Well," said Jack, pulling his mustache, perplexedly, "I should think the former."

"Moreover, the dragon, as he has been traditionally pictured by the Chinese and Japanese, for thousands of years, is, making due allowance for the low state of art among those people, a very graphic representation of a Saurian."

"So he is," cried Jack. "I never thought of that before."

"Now, the only remaining question," went on Charley, pinching a new segar before he lighted it, "it this—has the Saurian lived down to our time? In remote and primeval regions, such as you still find, occasionally, in South America and

Africa; in those vast morasses, which, geologically speaking, are like the earliest formations, it is yet possible—is it not?—that Saurians, that is dragons, may be found."

"If you put it in that way," cried Jack, "egad! you may be more than half right."

"More than half right?" thundered Charley. "I know I am right, altogether. Why, I've both seen and shot a dragon."

"Shot a dragon!" cried Jack, jumping from his chair, as if a bullet had hit him.

The wonder and amazement were not confined to Jack. The most eager curiosity—a curiosity that was half incredulous, I must confess—was in every countenance, as Charley, coolly knocking the ashes from his segar, and looking steadily at each of us in succession, went on.

"It was down on the western coast of Africa, mind you," he said, "a good way south of the Bight of Benin, where we had been driven by stress of weather, that I saw the monster. I was, at that time, supercargo on the good barque Samaritan, Bob Cushman being master and principal owner. Bob was of a first-rate old Boston sea-faring family, and had just been getting married, and his wife, as plucky a girl as ever lived, insisted on going out with him. We had a charming time, for a while; fair winds; everything we could desire. At last a gale struck us, that lasted, off and on, for nearly three weeks. In all that time we didn't get a solitary observation. When the storm had blown itself out, we found ourselves hundreds of miles from our course, and had nothing to do but to beat back, with baffling winds, no end of thunder-storms, and beastly, hot calms!

"Two months passed in this way. Finally we sighted land, and as we were nearly out of water, and two-thirds of our crew were down with fever, we ran for it at once, though we knew it was the fever-cursed African coast.

"We dropped anchor in a swollen, muddy, swirling river, with mangroves coming close down to the water's edge, and millions of monkeys chattering in the dense forest on either side; and the next evening, manning a boat with what of our crew was left fit for duty, we set forth to look for fresh water. So short-handed were we, that, when we mustered finally for this expedition, there wasn't a single able-bodied man we could leave behind with Bob's wife. But she, brave girl, said it didn't matter. 'You'll not be gone more than a day or two,' she declared, 'and I don't mind being left alone for that time. Fortunately there are no natives about here to do one harm.'

"We took the flood-tide, as the moon rose, and pulled steadily up stream.

"About an hour after midnight, we came to a high bluff, and landing at its foot, found a delicious spring, which bubbled up, clear and cool, amid luxuriant grasses and flowers, that reminded us of dear, old New England. We had taken soundings, all the way along, and found there was depth of water enough to bring the barque up to the bluff; so, resting till the tide turned, we started again for the mouth of the river with the ebb.

"It was a sight of extraordinary beauty. We, who live in northern climes, have no idea of the splendor of the heavens, in the tropics. The larger stars come out as brilliant as New England moons, and the moon is as bright almost as the sun here, only more silvery. The banks, on either hand, were covered with luxuriant vegetation: great mangroves that sent their contorted, snake-like roots far out into the river; gigantic trees, covered with long, trailing moss, or hung with huge leaves, that flapped, silently, in the still night-air, like the wings of weird birds. The day was just breaking, as we entered the reach of the river, where the barque lay moored; a close, sultry, foggy morning, like an August one at home, only a hundred times intensified.

"Poor Bob had been nervous and excited, ever since we had left the bluff. He had a presentiment, he said, that something was going to happen to his wife; and he urged the men, continually, to greater speed, though the poor fellows, tired out with their long pull, were already doing their best. It was with a cry of joy, therefore, that I saw the black hull of the barque, with its tracery of yards and rigging above, standing out, sharp and clean, against the gray, western sky, in which the wan moon was just setting. But I had hardly uttered the hurrah, when Bob clutched me wildly by the arm, and cried hoarsely. 'Look, look! Great heavens! what is that?'

"I followed his horror-struck gaze, and saw a sight that froze my very blood. Lying in the slime of the shore, between us and the barque, but much closer to the latter than to our boat, wallowed a vast monster, nameless in shape, that, at this instant, raised its repulsive head, and seeming to discern the ship for the first time, began to put its huge bulk in motion, as if to devour this new-found prey. As it rose from the mud and reeds of the shore, its vast proportions and unsightly figure became distinctly visible. Half-crocodile, half-elephant in body, with a large, tapering, scaly tail, and with a neck like a giraffe's, that swayed to and fro, as it waddled along, it would have been less an object of disgust, if it had not inspired such unspeakable horror. Its legs, and the claws at the end of them, were more than fins, and were yet not feet. Misshapen, undeveloped, terrible, gigantic, it rolled, as it were, along, leaving a great furrow in the mud behind it. All this time, its enormous head, in which glittered two large, fiery-red eyes, swung from side to side, as a horse's when weaving, as stable-boys call it; and its hideous mouth, filled with steel-like teeth, opened and shut, with eager appetite, and a snap that we could hear even at our distance.

"It soon reached the water, and, sliding in, began to swim awkwardly, yet swiftly, toward the barque. For a moment, notwithstanding its apparent intention, I had hoped it was not amphibious, and that, therefore, terrible as it looked, the vessel and its precious freight would be safe from it. But this illusion could be indulged in no longer. The monster was so much nearer the ship than we were, that, long before we could get alongside, its mighty jaws would be crunching the timbers like eggshells. Nor was this all. Even if we reached the barque, what could we do against such an adversary? All this rushed through my mind, as the unhappy husband, at my side, groaned, 'Oh! can nothing be done?'

"Nothing done? It was certain death, but we would, I said to myself, at least die heroically. I never went on any expedition without my rifle, and my friend was also armed. He had clutched his gun, as he spoke, and though the range was a long one, took aim, and fired. The ball hit the monster, but without seriously injuring him. I saw it glance off from his scaly hide. He turned, however, to see from what quarter his assailants came, and discovering us, wheeled his enormous bulk around, and cresting his neck and head high above the water, made rapidly for us, with eyes flashing with rage. I fired, almost instantly, taking his eyes for a mark, hoping in this way to reach the brain. But his incessant, undulatory movements made it impossible for me to be sure in my aim, and I had the horror of seeing that my shot had not even touched the dragon, for such I now knew the animal to be.

"Both rifles, by this time, were discharged, and as neither was a breech-loader, the monster would, almost certainly, be upon us, before we could re-load.

" 'Turn and pull away, it is our only chance,' I cried. 'A stern-chase is a long one, and it will give some time to re-load.' But the boat remained motionless, and glancing around, I saw that part of the crew were cowering in the bottom, paralyzed, and that the others had frantically leaped overboard; reason and courage, in what were otherwise brave and intelligent fellows, having given way in the face of this appalling and unheard-of danger. 'Load, load, Bob,' I shouted at this, 'and give it to him again; he must have a weak spot somewhere.'

"My answer was the click of the hammer, as Bob drew it back to put a cap on his rifle, and immediately after came the sharp, ringing sound of the ball as it sped on its way. I did not venture to look up, for I was ramming my own ball home, but I knew from the terrible cry of my friend, that his fire had proved as ineffectual, this time, as before. In a flash, all that depended on my next shot, the last probably that I should ever discharge, blazed, vivid and intense, before me. As in a magic-lantern I saw, in succession, the awful scenes. Once having dispatched us, there would be nothing to prevent his wreaking his rage on the barque. The vision of what would happen there almost unmanned me. But the noise of the monster, close at hand, like the quick paddling of a ferry-boat, stimulated me afresh. I had now got my ball home; it was but a moment's work to cap the nipple; then I lifted the rifle, and glanced along its shining barrel, feeling as if I had a thousand lives beating in my veins, and was willing to sell them all. 'Fire, fire, for God's sake, fire!' cried the husband, as I paused in this position. But I had resolved I would not fire, till I saw, at least, a chance of hitting a vulnerable part, or till the huge beast was actually upon us. Already this last contingency was close at hand. I could hear the noise of the creature breathing, and feel his hot breath; the water around us was, even now, swirling and eddying before the disturbance created by his vast circumference. At that instant, as he raised his huge head angrily, waving it from side to side, I saw what seemed a thinner fold of skin, just where the neck and breast met—you see the same in a tortoise—a fold that grew thinner yet as it was distended by the act of stretching out the neck and head. Here, if anywhere, was a vital entrance, for the heart lay directly behind it. Quick as thought my barrel sought it; the hammer fell; the shot rang out on the sultry air. 'Hurrah!' I shouted, in uncontrollable excitement, as I saw the blood spout from the wound, dyeing the water all around. Instantly the head fell flat on the tide, with a swashing sound; the mighty body rolled over on its side; and then the dragon floated past our boat, the horrible fins and tail thrashing the water in the death-agony.

"I turned to look at my friend. He had fallen, in a dead faint, across the tiller-ropes.

"Well," continued Charley, drawing a long breath, "of course we made for the barque, immediately. The happiest moment, I think, of all my life was when we leaped on deck, and found everything safe. Bob's pretty wife was still asleep; she had not even heard of the monster; and thank heaven! she never saw him either, or he might have haunted her dreams for weeks. As for us, we got up anchor at once, and made sail. 'Better go on half allowance of water for weeks,' said Bob, 'and be short-handed all the way to Shanghai, than stay another hour in this Inferno.'

"But I have since regretted that we did not remain long enough to bring away the head of the monster, or secure some other trophy of him. I could then have proved what you seem to doubt—that I shot THE LAST DRAGON."

George Sand

Fairy Dust

The French novelist Amantine Lucile Aurore Dupin, known as GEORGE SAND (1804-1876), *wove the earth sciences into some of her later work, most notably in the mineralogical adventure* Laura, voyage dans le cristal *(1864). Coupling an emphasis on careful scientific observation with a vision of the "active, dynamic, and mysterious" nature of life on earth, Sand's short story "Fairy Dust" is a phantasmagorical geological fairy tale.*[1] *As such, it belongs to a rich tradition of nineteenth-century writing, mostly for children, which used the imagery and anthropomorphic devices of fairy tales to enchant and explain scientific processes.*[2] *The story appeared as "La Fée poussière" in the newspaper* Le Temps *in August 1875 before being collected the following year in Sand's* Contes d'une grand-mère *(Tales of a Grandmother). This anonymous English translation was published in the November 1891 issue of the* Strand Magazine, *subtitled "A Story for Children."*

A LONG time ago—a very long time—I was young, and often heard people complain of a troublesome little creature who made her way in by the window, after she had been driven out at the door. She was so light and so tiny that she might have been said to float rather than to walk, and my parents compared her to a little fairy. The servants detested her, and sent her flying

1 Manon Mathias, *Vision in the Novels of George Sand* (Oxford: Oxford University Press, 2016), 106.
2 For the British side of this tradition, see Melanie Keene, *Science in Wonderland: The Scientific Fairy Tales of Victorian Britain* (Oxford: Oxford University Press, 2015).

with their dusting brushes; but they had no sooner dislodged her from one resting-place than she re-appeared at another.

She was always dressed in a slatternly trailing grey gown, and a sort of veil which the least breath of wind sent whirling about her head with its yellowish dishevelled locks.

Seeing her so persecuted made me take pity on her, and I willingly allowed her to rest herself in my little garden, though she oppressed my flowers a great deal. I talked with her, but without ever being able to draw from her a single word of common sense. She wished to touch everything, saying she was doing no harm. I got scolded for tolerating her, and when I had allowed her to come too near me, I was sent to wash myself and change my clothes, and was even threatened with being called by her name.

It was such a bad name that I dreaded it greatly. She was so dirty that some said she slept on the sweepings of the houses and streets; and that was why she was called Fairy Dust.

"Why are you so dirty?" I asked her, one day, when she wanted to kiss me.

"You are a stupid to be afraid of me," she answered, laughingly; "you belong to me, and resemble me more than you think. But you are a child, the slave of ignorance, and I should waste my time by trying to make you understand."

"Come," I said, "you seem inclined to talk sense at last. Explain to me what you have just said."

"I can't talk to you here," she replied. "I have too much to say to you, and, as soon as I settle down in any part of your house I am brushed away with contempt; but, if you wish to know who I am, call me three times to-night as soon as you fall asleep."

That said, she hurried away, uttering a hearty laugh, and I seemed to see her dissolve into a mist of gold, reddened by the setting sun.

When I was in bed that night I thought of her just as I was going to sleep.

"I've dreamed all that," I said to myself, "or else that little old creature is a mad thing. How can I possibly call her when I am asleep?"

I fell off to sleep, and presently dreamed that I called her; I am not sure that I did not even call to her aloud, three times, "Fairy Dust! Fairy Dust! Fairy Dust!"

At the same moment I was transported into an immense garden, in the midst of which stood an enchanted palace, and on the threshold of this marvellous dwelling stood awaiting me a lady resplendent with youth and beauty, dressed in magnificent festal clothes.

I flew to her, and she kissed me, saying—

"Well, do you recognise Fairy Dust!"

"No, not in the least, madame," I answered, "and I think you must be making fun of me."

"I am not making fun of you at all," she replied, "but as you are not able to understand what I say to you, I am going to show you a sight which will appear strange, and which I will make as brief as possible. Follow me!"

She led me into the most beautiful part of her residence. It was a little limpid lake, resembling a green diamond set in a ring of flowers, in which were sporting fish of all hues of orange and cornelian, Chinese amber-coloured carp, black and white swans, exotic ducks decked in jewels, and, at the bottom, pearl and purple shells, bright-coloured aquatic salamanders; in short, a world of living wonders, gliding and plunging above a bed of silvery sand, on which were growing all sorts of water-plants, one more charming than another. Around this vast basin were ranged in several circles a colonnade of porphyry, with alabaster capitals. The entablature was made of the most precious minerals, and almost disappeared under a growth of clematis, jessamine, briony and honeysuckle, amid which a thousand birds made their nests. Roses of all tints and all scents were reflected in the water as well as the porphyry columns and the beautiful statues of Parian marble placed under the arcades. In the midst of the basin a fountain threw a thousand jets of diamonds and pearls.

The bottom of the architectural amphitheatre opened upon flower-beds shaded by giant trees, loaded to their summits with blossoms and fruit, their branches interlaced with trailing vines, forming above the porphyry colonnade a colonnade of verdure and flowers.

There the Fairy made me seat myself with her at the entrance to a grotto, whence there issued a melodious cascade, flowing over fresh moss sparkling with diamond drops of water.

"All that you see there is my work," she said to me; "all that is made of dust. It is by the shaking of my gown in the clouds that I have furnished all the materials of this paradise. My friend Fire, who threw them into the air, has taken them back to re-cook them, to crystallise or compact them, after which my servant Wind took them about with him amid the moisture and electricity of the clouds, and then cast them upon the earth; this wide plain has then arisen from my fecund substance, and rain has made sands and grass of it, after having made rocks into porphyries, marbles, and metals of all sorts."

I listened without understanding, and I thought that the Fairy was continuing to mystify me. How she could have made the earth out of dust still passes my comprehension; that she could have made marble and granites and other minerals merely by shaking the skirt of her gown, I could not believe. But I did not dare to contradict her, though I turned involuntarily towards her to see whether she was speaking seriously of such an absurdity.

What was my surprise to find she was no longer behind me! but I heard her voice, seemingly coming from under the ground, calling me. At the same time I also passed under ground without being able to resist, and found myself in a terrible place where all was fire and flame. I had heard tell of the infernal region; I thought that was it. Lights, red, blue, green, white, violet—now pale, now swelling, replaced daylight, and, if the sun penetrated to this place, the vapours which arose from the furnace made it wholly invisible.

Formidable sounds, sharp hisses, explosions, claps of thunder, filled this clouded cavern in which I felt myself enclosed. In the midst of all this I perceived little Fairy Dust, who had gone back to her dirty colourless dress. She came and went, working, pushing, piling, clutching, pouring out I know not what acids; in a word, giving herself up to an incomprehensible labour.

"Don't be afraid," she said to me, in a voice that rose above the deafening noises of this Tartarus. "You are here in my laboratory. Don't you know anything about machinery?"

"Nothing at all," I shouted, "and I don't want to learn about it in such a place as this."

"Yes, you wanted to know, and you must resign yourself to me. It is very pleasant to live on the surface of the earth, with flowers, birds, and domesticated animals, to bathe in still waters, to eat nice-tasting fruits, to walk upon carpets of greensward and daisies. You imagined that life has always existed in that way, under such blessed conditions. It is time you should learn something about the beginning of things, and of the power of Fairy Dust, your grandmother, your mother, and your nurse."

As she spoke the little creature made me roll with her into the depths of the abysm, through devouring flames, frightful explosions, acrid black smoke, metals in fusion, lavas vomiting hideously, and all the terrors of volcanic eruption.

"These are my furnaces," she said, "the underground where my provisions elaborate themselves. You see, it is a good place for a mind disencumbered of the shell called a body. You have left yours in your bed, and your mind alone is with me. So you may touch and clutch primary matter. You are ignorant of chemistry; you do not yet know of what this matter is made, nor by what mysterious operation what appears here under the aspect of solid bodies come from a gaseous body which has shone in space, first as a nebula and later as a beaming sun. You are a child; I cannot initiate you into the great secrets of creation, and there is a long time yet to be passed before your professors themselves will know them. But I can show you the products of my culinary art. All here is somewhat confused for you. Let us mount a stage. Hold the ladder, and follow me."

A ladder, of which I could not perceive either the bottom or the top, stood before us. I followed the Fairy, and found myself in darkness, but I then noticed that she herself was wholly luminous and radiant as a torch. I then observed enormous deposits of oozy paste, blocks of whitish crystal and immense waves of black and shining vitreous matter, which the Fairy took up and crumbled between her fingers; then she piled the crystal in little heaps, and mixed all with the moist paste, and placed the whole on what she was pleased to call a gentle fire.

"What dish are you going to make of that?" I asked.

"A dish necessary to your poor little existence," she replied. "I am making granite,—that is to say, with dust I make the hardest and most resisting of stones; it needs that to enclose Cocytus and Phlegethon. I make also various mixtures of the same elements. Here is what is shown to you under barbarous names—gneiss, the quartzes, the talcs, the micas, *et cetera*. Of all that which comes from my dust, I, later on, make other dusts with new elements, which will then be slates, sand, and gravel. I am skilful and patient; I pulverise unceasingly to reagglomerate. Is not flour the basis of all cakes? At the present time I imprison my furnaces, contriving for them some necessary vents, so that they may not burst. We will go above and see what is going on. If you are tired, you may take a nap, for it will take me a little to accomplish what I am going to do."

I lost all consciousness of time, and when the Fairy waked me:

"You have been sleeping a pretty considerable number of ages!" she said.

"How many, Madame Fairy?"

"You must ask that of your professors," she replied, laughingly. "Let us go on up the ladder."

She made me mount several stages through divers deposits, where I saw her manipulate the rust of metals, of which she made chalk, marl, clay, slate, jasper; and as I questioned her as to the origin of metals:

"You want to know a great deal about it," she said. "Your inquirers may explain many phenomena by fire and water; but could they know what was passing between earth and heaven when all my dust, cast by wind from the abyss, has formed solid clouds, which clouds of water have rolled in their stormy whirl, which thunder has penetrated with its mysterious loadstone, and which the stronger winds have thrown upon a terrestrial surface in torrential rains? There is the origin of the first deposits. You are going to witness these marvellous transformations."

We mounted higher, and came to chalks, marbles, and banks of limestone enough to build a city as big as the entire globe. And as I was wondering at what she was able to produce by sifting, agglomerating, metamorphosing, and baking, she said to me:

"All that is nothing; you are going to see a great deal more than that—you are going to see life, already hatched in the middle of these stones."

She approached a basin wide as a sea, and, plunging her arms into it, drew from it—first, strange plants, then animals, stranger still, which were as yet half plants; then beings, free and independent of one another, living shells; then, at last, fish, which she made leap, saying as she did so:

"That's what Dame Dust knows how to produce, when she pleases, at the bottom of water. But there's something better than that. Turn round and look at the shore."

I turned. The calcar and all its components, mixed with flint and clay, had formed on the surface a fine brown and rich dust, out of which had sprung fibrous plants of singular form.

"That is vegetable earth," said the Fairy. "Wait a little while, and you will see trees growing."

I then saw an arborescent vegetation rise rapidly from the ground and people itself with reptiles and insects, while on the shore unknown creatures crawled and darted about, and caused me great terror.

"These animals will not alarm you on the earth of the future," said the Fairy. "They are destined to manure it with their remains. There are not yet any human beings here to fear them."

"Hold!" I cried; "here is a world of monsters that shock me! Here is your earth belonging to these devouring creatures who live upon one another. Do you need all these massacres and all these stupidities to make us a muck-heap? I can understand their not being good for anything else, but I can't understand a creation so rich in animated forms to do nothing and to leave nothing worth anything behind it."

"Manure is something, if it is not everything; the conditions it will create will be favourable to different beings who will succeed those on which you are looking."

"And which will disappear in their turn, I know that. I know that creation will go on improving itself up to the creation of Man—at least, that is, I think, what I have been told. But I had not pictured to myself this prodigality of life and destruction, which terrifies me and fills me with repugnance; these hideous forms, these gigantic amphibia, these monstrous crocodiles, and all these crawling or swimming beasts which seem to live only to use their teeth and devour one another."

My indignation highly amused Fairy Dust.

"Matter is matter," she replied, "it is always logical in its operations. The human mind is not—and you have proved it—you who live by eating charming birds, and a crowd of creatures more beautiful and intelligent than these. Have I to teach you that there is no production possible without permanent destruction, and would you like to reverse the order of nature?"

"Yes, I would—I should like that all should go well from the first day. If Nature is a great fairy she might have done without all these abominable experiments, and made a world in which we should all have been angels, living by mind only, in the bosom of an unchangeable and always beautiful creation."

"The great fairy Nature has higher views," replied Dame Dust. "She does not intend to stop at the things of which you know. She is always at work and inventing. For her, for whom there is no such thing as the suspension of life, rest would be death. If things did not change the work of the King of the Genii would be ended, and this king, who is incessant and supreme activity, would end with his work. The world which you see, and to which you will return presently when your vision of the past has faded away, this world of man, which you think is better than that of the ancient animals, this world with which you yet are not satisfied, since you wish to live eternally in a pure spiritual condition, this poor planet, still in a state of infancy, is destined to transform itself infinitely. The future will make of you all—feeble human creatures that you are— fairies and genii possessing science, reason, and goodness. You have seen what I have shown to you, that these first drafts of life, representing simply instinct, are nearer to you than you are to that which will some day be the reign of mind in the earth which you inhabit. The occupants of that future world will then have the right to despise you, as you now despise the world of the great saurians."

"Oh! if that is so," I replied, "if all that I have seen of the past will make me think the better of the future, let me see more that is new."

"And, above all," said the Fairy, "don't let us too much despise the past, for fear of committing the ingratitude of despising the present. When the great Spirit of life used the materials which furnished it, it did marvels from the first day. Look at the eyes of this monster which your learned men have called the ichthyosaurus."

"They are as large as my head, and frighten me."

"They are very superior to yours. They are at once long and short-sighted at will. They see prey at great distances as with a telescope, and when it is quite near, by a simple change of action, they see it perfectly at its true distance without needing spectacles. At that moment of creation nature had but one purpose: to make a thinking animal. It gave to this creature organs marvellously appropriate to its wants. Don't you think it made a very pretty beginning—are you not struck by it? In this way it will proceed from better to better, with all the beings which are to succeed those you now see. Those which appear to you poor, ugly, pitiful, are yet prodigies of adaptation to the place in the midst of which they have manifested themselves."

"And, like the others, they think of nothing but eating!"

"Of what would you have them think? The earth has no wish to be admired. The sky, which exists to-day and for ever, will continue to exist without the aspirations and prayers of tiny living creatures adding anything to the splendour and majesty of its laws. The fairy of your little planet, no doubt, knows the great First Cause; but if she is ordered to make a being who shall perceive or guess that Cause, it will be in obedience to the law of time—that law of which you can form no idea, because you live too short a space to appreciate its operations. You think those operations slow, yet they are carried on with a bewildering rapidity. I will free your mind from its natural weakness, and show you in rotation the results of innumerable centuries. Look, and don't cavil any more, but profit by my kindness to you."

I felt that the Fairy was right, and I looked, with all my eyes, at the succession of aspects of the earth. I saw the birth and death of vegetables and of animals become more and more vigorous from instinct, and more and more agreeable or imposing in form. In proportion as the ground decked itself with productions more nearly resembling those of our days, the inhabitants of this widespread garden, in which great accidents were incessantly transforming, appeared to become less eager to destroy each other, and more careful of their progeny. I saw them construct dwelling-places for the use of their families, and exhibit attachment for localities, so much so that, from moment to moment, I saw a world fade away, and a new world arise in its place, like the changing of the scenes in a fairy-play.

"Rest awhile," the Fairy said to me, "for, without suspecting it, you have traversed a good many thousands of centuries, and Mr. Man is going to be born when the reign of Mr. Monkey has been completed."

I once more fell asleep, quite overcome by fatigue, and when I awoke I found myself in the midst of a grand hall in the palace of the Fairy, who had again become young, beautiful, and splendidly dressed.

"You see all these charming things, and all this charming company?" she said to me. "Well, my child, all that is *dust!* These walls of porphyry and marble are dust, molecules kneaded and roasted to a turn. These buildings of cut stone are the dust of lime or of granite, brought about by the same process. These crystal lustres are fine sand baked by the hands of men in imitation of the work of Nature. These porcelain and china articles are the powder of feldtspar, the kaolin of which the Chinese have taught us the use. These diamonds in which the dancers are decked are coal-dust crystallised. These pearls are phosphate of lime which the oyster exudes into its shell. Gold and all the metals have no other origin than the assemblage, well heaped, well melted, well heated, and well cooled, of infinitesimal molecules. These beautiful vegetables, these flesh-coloured roses, these stainless lilies, these gardenias which embalm the air, are born of dust which I prepared for them; and these people who dance and smile at the sound of those musical instruments, these living creatures *par excellence*, who are called persons, they also—don't be offended—are born of me, and will be returned to me."

As she said that, the hall and the palace disappeared. I found myself with the Fairy in a field of corn. She stooped, and picked up a stone in which there was a shell encrusted.

"There," she said, "in a fossil state is a being which I showed you in the earliest ages of life. What is it now?—phosphate of lime. Reducing it to dust, people make manure of it for land that is too flinty. You see, Man is beginning to understand one thing—that the master to study is Nature."

She crumbled the shell into powder, and scattered it on the cultivated soil, saying:

"This will come back to my kitchen. I spread destruction to make the germ spring. It is so of all dusts, whether they be plants, animals, or persons. They are death, after having been life, and there is nothing sad in it, since, thanks to me, they always begin again to live after having been dead. Farewell! You greatly admired my ball dress: here is a piece of it, which you may examine at your leisure."

All disappeared, and, when I opened my eyes, I found myself in my bed. The sun had risen, and sent a bright ray towards me. I looked for the piece of stuff which the Fairy had put into my hand: it was nothing but a little heap of dust; but my mind was still under the charm of the dream, and it gave to my senses the power of distinguishing the smallest atom of this dust.

I was filled with wonderment. There was everything in it: air, water, sun, gold, diamonds, ashes, the pollen of flowers, shells, pearls, the dust of butterflies' wings, of thread, of wax, of iron, of wood, and of many microscopic bodies; but in the midst of this mixture of imperceptible refuse, I saw fermenting I know not what life of undistinguishable beings, that appeared to be trying to fix themselves to something, to hatch or to transform themselves, all confounded in a golden mist, or in the roseate rays of the rising sun.

Amanda Theodosia Jones

From Saurian to Seraph

*It is commonly assumed that the discoveries of geologists and paleon-
tologists in the nineteenth century must have been highly damaging to
contemporary Christian faith. Instead, these discoveries often provided
a new language for religious reflection. Such a language is at work in
this poem by the American spiritualist, philanthropist, and canned goods
entrepreneur* AMANDA THEODOSIA JONES (1835-1914). *Although
the narrative is a tale of redemption, Quakerism, ghostly visitations, the
Underground Railroad, and the Civil War, at its heart lies a metaphor
of prehistory—of the "old Saurian age." The narrator, a blacksmith,
relates the action of his life to a passing woman, illustrating how he
has struggled to harness the crude dinosaurian side of his nature in the
name of more angelic pursuits. The poem, which a reviewer in the popular* Century Magazine *compared to the work of Elizabeth Barrett
Browning, appeared in Jones's anonymous 1882 collection* A Prairie
Idyl and Other Poems.[1]

I.

'T WAS a poor blacksmith did the work before;
   The pony interferes: you'll please get down;
I served apprenticeship seven years or more
   In London, ere Victoria wore the crown,
And I can shoe a horse with any man.
   [*Whoa there! stand still!*] . . . I saw you on the road;
You ride as well as any lady can,—
   And he's a trim beast, worthy such a load.

1 "A Prairie Idyl," *Century Illustrated Magazine*, 25 (1882-83), 151.

II.

Fine day for riding: how the sun laughs out!
　　Look at those rapids, glittering down the fall.
And have you heard the birds? they shout and shout—
　　Sun, birds, and waters—well, I love them all.
Yet once I was a brute: what was a bird,
　　That I should stay to watch him in his flight?
Forty-two battles I've been in, and heard
　　My horse's hoofs clang hard through every fight.

III.

Oh, then I had rich times! then I was proud!
　　You should have seen: the sabre in my hand
Was just one red, and dripping like a cloud!
　　There never was a life so glad and grand.
But when the last ball's ricochet made rout,
　　And the last shell tore up the bloody sod,
I used to call my corps of blacksmiths out
　　And drive the nails till every beast was shod.

IV.

"Rest?" Bless you! have such creatures need of rest?
　　Look, girl! you've heard of that old Saurian age
When scaly monsters crowded breast to breast
　　And tusk to tusk in one destroying rage?
I do believe that mad, blind, battling force
　　That smote so at the bass of earth's great harp,
Through finer ages rolled its cloudy course,
　　And shook my frame with thunder swift and sharp.

V.

For there's a law that sums every cycle—gives
　　Its full, stern impulse to the life beyond:
And every spirit, weak or strong, that lives

Is nerved to feel such urgings and respond.
Oh, they refine, I grant, through starry fire!
The Saurian rage that lights a seraph's eyes
Is just that still white flame that sends him higher,
With "Alleluia!" challenging the skies.

VI.

That for the seraph: but for me you know,
Why I was in the sloughs—a very brute!
In stifling airs my soul began to grow,
Mire-clogged—as all God's grandeur to refute!
Yet more than Saurian in spite of all:
I felt the winds blow cooler now and then;
Down the wide wastes heard far sweet voices call,
And knew my beasts and dimly yearned for men.

VII.

I'll drop my metaphors: you'll understand
I served ten years because I loved to slay;
And having fought, was fed. Oh, it was grand!
My brutish blood ran richer day by day.
I had a Quaker mother . . . well, she died:
I think till then she never lived—in me.
My father and myself fought side by side,
Grim battle-mates: small chance for her, you see.

VIII.

But after death I saw her—where she came,
A spirit pale, right through my furnace-heat:
"Such fire and no one warmed? O son, for shame!"
And I fell down and trembled at her feet.
That proved me man; for mark, no beast will wake
At call of angels! I began to stir,
And question of the sloughs what way to take
If I might rise and follow after her.

IX.

I left the service when my time was out,
    And crossed from Canada to settle down;
But I could only drift and drift about,
    And wander drearily from town to town.
One day it chanced I came upon a crowd
    Mobbing an orator—a boorish gang:
"Bring on your rotten eggs!" one called aloud;
    "We'll hear no Abolitionist harangue."

X.

Well, I went in for sport: I filled my hat
    And shot out straight (I never miss my aim);
It struck the man between the eyes,—at that
    A laugh went roaring upward like a flame.
Just then a hand fell softly on my head:
    "My man, has thee no better wares to vend?"
I turned (an egg half-raised): "Let be!" he said;
    "Thee doesn't know what thee is doing, friend."

XI.

Oh, how ashamed I was!—dyed red clear through!
    I felt as small as any crawling worm.
Meantime a shower of stones above me flew:
    "Yon fellow'll flinch," I thought; but he stood firm.
Then like a lion startled with the hunt,
    Whose sudden voice will strike the Arabs mute,
All quivering wrath, I bounded to the front:
    The very man in me unleashed the brute!

XII.

What happened further? Nay, I hardly know!
    I meant just slaughter. "Touch him if you like!"
I roared: "Come on! I'll give you blow for blow!

Look! here's a British fist! now feel it strike!"
I routed them—the cowards! made them fly
    Howling as if the world was like to end.
And then I found my Quaker: "Well," said I;
    "I've sold my wares!" He laughed: "Thee's valiant, friend;

XIII.

"Thee'd better keep with us; we'll do thee good."
    And so they did: A truer life I found,
Caught at the golden lines of brotherhood
    And scrambled from the mire to safer ground.
You see those Quaker mothers took me in,
    And fed me, starving, with the holy bread
Christ brake among the twelve; and what can win
    Like those dear words the lowly Master said?

XIV.

And there I learned the story of the slave
    (That earthquake-tremor sure to rend the land);
And, signing me that I should haste to save,
    In every cloud I saw my mother's hand;
In every wind I heard her voice: *"My son:*
    And will thy boasted strength but serve to slay?
Under the cross of labor, scourged, undone,
    They need thee who have fallen by the way."

XV.

So many years I kept the secret track,
    To guide those straying negroes into rest;
And when their masters followed, sent them back
    The poorer by a slave or two at best.
But sometimes, when pursuit was fierce and hot,
    I caught some cruel fellow with a grip,
And bound him hand and foot: I kept my shot

For bloodhounds—but I lent his slaves my whip.

XVI.

For I was brutal still: and yet I learned
    All Blackstone in those days, and much of Coke;
I read the histories where their battles burned,
    And laid me under Shakespeare's "gnarlèd oak,"
(Whose acorns sprout in every soil to make
    The round earth green!); loved Junius, Cicero,
And Whittier; made the sober Quakers quake
    For laughter, with my violin and bow.

XVII.

Meanwhile I took a wife;—for what's a man
    With all his loves at dry-rot in his heart?
Unseasoned timbers—bound to mar the plan
    And sink the ship, however fair the chart.
But a good wife is like a strong sweet breeze
    That searches in and out and keeps all right:
Ah, yes! and fills the sails till childly seas
    Leap up and clap their hands in sheer delight!

XVIII.

There's nothing like a wife; and mine's a queen.
    When from his egg that huge war-python crept,
She let me go; and yet if you had seen
    How hard it was, I think you would have wept.
But I—my happy heart beat fast and loud
    (Made greater by Love's ichor in the veins),
To share—my horse and I—through fire and cloud
    That world-wide rapture of the hurricanes.

XIX.

I never blame the Rebels: but be sure

I do not blame myself for shooting them.
There's not a wind in Heaven so cool and pure,
    It has not brushed some martyr's blazing hem!
There's not a waving flower throughout the skies
    So white, it is not rooted deep in mud!
Between the suns there's not a seraph flies
    That somehow, somewhere, did not wade in blood!

XX.

Why, even you—bright-glancing—you, who stand
    So lightly poised, like any forest-bird,
That if you did not urge me (voice and hand
    And ardent eye), I should not speak a word
For fear you'd soar! There'll come a time you'll set
    Those milky teeth—will clasp your girdle well,
And on the nearest stone the knife you'll whet
    To flay some scarlet dragon late from Hell!

XXI.

But, grander still, from out your gold you'll sift
    That sand of self, the whole deep mountain through:
Because of Love, such weights of care you'll lift,
    The sweat of blood will gather fast as dew.
GOD help you, girl! for all the deaths you'll dare;
    Wind, frost and flood, serpent and beast you'll greet:
Till one shall come and hale you by the hair
    Straight to the fagots! . . . There's the secret sweet.

XXII.

I've guessed it partly. Pausing in the fight
    One day, behold my mother standing near!
And all around her played such tongues of light
    As would have made the bravest martyr fear.
More pallid than the dead, and waving slow

Her hands toward the South: *"I bore thee, child,"*
She said, *"with bitter pangs: but thou shalt know*
   A larger grief than mine!"—and then she smiled.

XXIII.

Now, when my soul from that dread trance awoke
   (Low reeling in the saddle, reins all slack),
A man I loved came plunging through the smoke
   With half a score of Rebels on his track.
I flung between; I galloped to and fro;
   Broad sweeps of sabre barred the fell pursuit:
But so they took me prisoner; caged me so
   All bleeding; starved me as a jungle brute.

XXIV.

Two summers . . . "What of them?" Hush! never wish
   To read those inky tablets of the flood;
Down by the altar set no silver dish
   To catch the dripping of the bullock's blood;
Ask not of fires that drank all currents up,
   Aye, emptied out of the hollows of the sea!
Nor dare with those young lips to press the cup
   They drain who travail in Gethsemane!

XXV.

They brought me home, an idiot, to my wife;
   My children kissed me, and I did not know.
Just one last drop was in the springs of life,
   And long they watched if any wave could flow.
It came at last—slow rising to the brim,
   The deep sweet fountain drawn through veins of Death,
Out of that dear, abundant Heart of Him
   Most Calm, who lives all life, who breathes all breath.

XXVI.

And now I blow the coals, I pare the hoof
  (GOD labors; so must we); I come and go;
But when some lightning rends this rainy roof—
  An instant stroke (they say it will be so),—
Ah, then, all drenched and charred beneath, above
  All supple grace!—who knows what holy cheer
Of kisses me will greet? what whorls of Love
  Will fold me round, sphere rolled on rosy sphere?

XXVII.

This certain: That dread Power, so prone to waste,
  That bids the Saurian gnash devouring teeth,
The gunner plant his guns, the martyr haste
  To perish in the fagots' flaming sheath,
Nerves still some white and virile hand that flings
  Wide open all the gateways of the sky;
Rounds out some seraph's voice, the while he sings
  His "Holy, holy is the LORD MOST HIGH!"

May Kendall

Ballad of the Ichthyosaurus

*The Ichthyosaurus, or fish-lizard, had been unearthed by Mary
Anning at Lyme Regis in the early nineteenth century, and its notori-
ously cumbersome name became a byword for the strangeness of extinct
animals.[1] As this poem by* MAY KENDALL (1861-1943) *stresses, the
Ichthyosaurus's huge eye was commonly described as possessing a
functional perfection that contrasted with the animal's evolutionary
primitiveness. Kendall, an English author of poetry, fiction, and social
criticism, here seems to celebrate the intellectual superiority of humanity,
but her references to modern schooling, exams, universities, and famous
men of science suggest playful parallels with those fossil reptiles who
"dined, as a rule, on each other." The poem appeared anonymously in
the leading British humor magazine of the time,* Punch, *in February
1885. Although this musical ichthyosaur resides at the British Museum,
"in sweet Bloomsbury's halls," the Museum's natural history collections
had actually been relocated to the South Kensington district of London
several years earlier. This relocation was the brainchild of anatomist
Richard Owen, also mentioned in the poem.*

[The Ichthyosaurus laments his incomplete development and
imperfect education. He aspires to better things.]

I ABIDE in a goodly Museum
    Frequented by sages profound,

1 John Glendening, " 'The World-Renowned Ichthyosaurus': A Nineteenth-
Century Problematic and Its Representations," *Journal of Literature and Science*, 2 (2009), 23-47.

In a kind of a strange mausoleum,
    Where the beasts that have vanished abound,
There's a bird of the Ages Triassic
    With his antediluvian beak,
And many a reptile Jurassic,
    And many a monster antique!

Ere Man was developed, our brother,
    We swam, and we ducked, and we dived,
And we dined, as a rule, on each other.
    What matter, the toughest survived!
Our paddles were fins, and they bore us
    Through water,—in air we could fly;
But the brain of the Ichthyosaurus
    Was never a match for his eye!

The geologists, active and eager,
    Its excellence hasten to own,
And praise, with no eulogy meagre,
    The eye that is plated with bone!
"See how, with unerring precision,
    His prey through the waves he could spy;
Oh, wonderful organ of vision,
    Gigantic and beautiful eye!"

Then I listen in gloomy dejection,
    I gaze, and I wish I could weep
For what is mere visual perfection
    To Intellect, subtle and deep?
A loftier goal is before us,
    For higher endowments we sigh,
But—the brain of the Ichthyosaurus
    Was never a patch on his eye!

It owned no supreme constitution,

Was shallow, and simple, and plain,
While mark but the fair convolution
   And size of the Aryan brain!
'Tis furnished for School-Board inspections,
   And garnished for taking degrees,
And bulging in many directions,
   As every phrenologist sees.

Sometimes it explodes at high pressure
   In harsh, overwhelming demand,
But, plied in unmerciful measure,
   It's wonderful what it will stand!
In cottage, in college, and mansion
   Bear witness the girls and the boys,
How great are its powers of expansion,
   How very peculiar its joys!

O Brain that is bulgy with learning,
   O Wisdom of women and men,
O Maids for a First that are yearning,
   O Youths that are lectured by WREN!
You're acquainted with Pisces and Taurus
   And all sorts of beasts in the sky,
But the brain of the Ichthyosaurus
   Was never so good as his eye!

Reconstructed by DARWIN or OWEN
   We dwell in sweet Bloomsbury's halls,
But we couldn't have passed Little-go in
   The Schools; we'd have floundered in Smalls!
Though so cleverly people restore us
   We are bound to confess, with a sigh,
That the brain of the Ichthyosaurus
   Was *never* so good as his eye!

Constance Naden

Geological Epochs

A defiant thinker in many fields, English scientific writer and poet
CONSTANCE NADEN *(1858-1889) was fascinated by evolutionary
theory and its implications for ethics and faith.*[1] *Skeptical about religion
in general, Naden deals here with Christian attempts to reconcile the
six days of creation from the start of the Book of Genesis—traditionally
authored by Moses—with the conclusions of geologists and paleontologists. Reconcilers typically assumed that the "days" of Genesis represented long geological periods and pondered over the appropriate day in
which to place prehistoric animals like dinosaurs. These reconciliation
schemes had been controversial since long before Naden was born, but
in 1885 a new "Revised" version of the King James (or "Authorized")
Bible was produced, modernizing its language and making some con-
cessions to contemporary science. Naden had little patience for endeavors
like these. The same year, her response to the "Revised" Old Testament
appeared in the July issue of the periodical* Agnostic. *The irreverent
article questions the misleading language used neatly to dovetail Genesis
and fossil evidence, proposing instead a secular view of geohistory charac-
terized by the "ceaseless play of Protean forces."*

THE relation of the Revisers of the Authorised Version to their
work and to the public is not inaptly prefigured by a well-
known fable of Æsop, entitled "The Old Man and his Ass."
Or, perhaps, we had better seek an illustration less irreverently

---

1 Clare Stainthorp, *Constance Naden: Scientist, Philosopher, Poet* (Oxford:
Peter Lang, 2019).

suggestive. A skilled surgeon, whose professional education has been supplemented by wide experience and deep research, is required to perform a delicate and complex series of operations, involving a near approach to vital parts. But it is stipulated that he must act under the supervision of an ancient lady, very tender of heart, but knowing nothing whatever about the structure and functions of that or of any other organ. She shrieks at every incision; she is quite sure that it cannot be right to cut away the diseased flesh, or, at any rate, *all* of it; she thinks, for her own part, that so much meddling with Nature, and prying into what was meant to be secret, does more harm than good. She has an unexpressed idea that surgery, like art, is improper. And so the surgeon does as much as she will allow; furtively trying to deceive her Argus eyes and to do a little more.

The Revisers are in nearly as sad a predicament as our supposititious operator: their own consciences can scarcely be appeased by the marginal notes, nor have they entirely satisfied that theological Mrs. Grundy, whom we may call "Traditional Reverence."

This paper, however, is not intended to be a dissertation on the merits and shortcomings of the Revised Version. I only mean to take a text, and then to wander away from it with that delightful freedom which is allowed both to clerics and to critics. Probably all readers have turned with interest to the first chapter of Genesis, and, after noting that "waste" is substituted for "without form," in the description of the inchoate earth, have passed on to the next striking emendation: "And there was evening and there was morning, one day." That is my text.

Now, I do not wish to revive the miserable suit of "Moses *versus* Geology." The so-called "reconciliation" of Scripture with Science is a branch of special pleading admitting of much perverted ingenuity, and probably there will be advocates ready to take up the discredited cause so long as any can be found who will listen and reply. In matters theological a very little reason goes a very long way, and the British juryman is not especially careful in considering his verdict when "Guilty" or "Not Guilty" will involve no secular consequences; nothing, in fact, save Heaven or Hell. We need not wonder, then, that he has been contented to read the word "day" as signifying "epoch" or "cycle," and yet to find in the seventh day, when God rested "from all his work which he had made," a precedent for Sabbatarianism. But this assumption, so calmly made by (or rather *for*) the British juryman, affords food for serious thought as to his conceptions of Geology. Let us suppose that he is an intelligent specimen of his class, and that he has studied the subject in popular manuals, and perhaps a little in the field. He has been much interested in what he has read and seen, and the ideas he has formed are clear, pictorial, and dramatic. The successive "periods" pass before him like scenes in a tragedy, each having a definite beginning, middle, and end. Each, therefore, is fairly comparable to a day, brightening from morning till perfect noon, gradually dimming towards evening, and lost at last in night. Nothing could be more beautiful or more complete. There was a time, he will tell you, when the area which is now Europe was submerged beneath the sea. Shell-fish, strange tripartite Crustaceans, corals, and other branching organisms bearing flower-like cups, were the chief inhabitants of the waters. These were enshrined and preserved in strata of sand and gravel and mud, since consolidated into hard grey rocks. This period passed away with the life thereof; and then came the dawn of another age—an age of inland lakes, of estuaries, of shallow, brackish seas. Then flourished gigantic ferns and horse-tails and club-mosses, luxuriant conifers and cycads; while the seas were peopled by fishes covered with bony scales. Insects and other "creeping things" came into being, and near the margin of the lakes enormous toads disported themselves. Red sands were laid down in the morning and in the evening of the cycle; but the noon saw the forests and jungles and reedy deltas, which, in the process of time and of decay, formed our coal measures.

Yet another epoch dawned. Lizards, twenty feet long, paddled through the sea like fishes, raising long, slender, swan-like necks above the waters. Others flew through the air with bat-wings; and, at last, there appeared a genuine bird with feathers, retaining teeth and a peculiarly-constructed tail as reptilian reminiscences. Mammals, too, there were, chiefly or wholly marsupial. The materials deposited were very various—clays, sands, and limestones; and great beds of chalk were formed from the shell-like coverings of tiny animalculæ.

Next came a period when genera, and even species of plants and animals which survive at the present day, grew more and more abundant. An antiquated type of horse gradually made way for forms approximating to his living representative; the pachyderms and the ruminants began to diverge from a common stock; birds and insects multiplied. The plants assumed a more familiar aspect; traces remain of the fig, the maple, the hickory, even of the water-lily and buck-bean. In these times the Alps were upheaved; the continent of Europe assumed something of its present shape; but its climate was tropical, slowly declining towards the eventide of the secular day.

Our modern times were ushered in by a glacial age. Europe was covered with a great sheet of ice down to the fiftieth parallel of latitude. Britain, as far south as Bristol, was glaci-ated as Greenland is now. After the ice-sheet had retired man appeared, living at first in dens and caves of the earth, and using implements of rough stone; but gradually learning to build houses and to forge tools of bronze and iron.

Such is a fair outline of the geological ideas which our intel-ligent Briton may be expected to form. If he goes out into the field, he finds them confirmed. Where deposition has gone on with little or no interruption, the formations overlie each other evenly, which he interprets as evidence of geological daytime. When deposition has ceased for a time, and the rocks have been upheaved and partly worn away in the interval, the newer strata will lie on the edges of the older ones, and this, perhaps, he will consider as the record of a geological night. It is true that the "periods" which I have described do not correspond in their essential characters with the "days" of Genesis; but every Sunday-schoolboy ought to know that nothing is impossible with a commentator. By judiciously dividing and ingeniously suppressing and supposititiously supplementing, and otherwise manipulating the testimony of the rocks, he can force them to repeat a tale which, at first hearing, may seem to bear out his theory. But let not the jurors make up their minds till they have heard the cross-examination.

What, then, do these geological "periods" represent? But, before trying to answer this question, let me mark the lines on which our investigation and reasoning must proceed. Every one, whether bent upon reconciling reason with "revelation," or convinced that such reconciliation is impossible, must accept at least the broad principles on which are founded all sober scientific theories; otherwise he puts himself outside the pale of argument, and can hope for no hearers save the fantastic and the ignorant. We start from the truism that like effects are produced by like causes, with its corollary, that if, in our experience, a certain phenomenon is always preceded by a certain process, we are right in assuming, wherever we find the phenomenon, that the process has taken place. If we walk on the seashore at low tide, and pick up shells and seaweed, we are quite sure that they have been brought there by the sea, though they are now many yards above its margin. We know, too, that the sea has rounded these pebbles which now lie high and dry, and has laid down this smooth yellow sand. If we were told that the seaweed had originally grown in a garden, or that the pebbles had been polished by a lapidary, who had afterwards scattered them about for his own amusement, we should entertain a strong private opinion as to the sanity of our informant. Just in the same way, we are obliged to interpret geological phenomena by the every-day processes which we see going on around us. Following this clue, we find that water has been the chief agent in the formation of the stratified rocks. In the form of rain and rivers, it bears away the materials of the land and lays them on the floor of the sea in horizontal beds. Marine animals and plants die, and fall to the bottom, and are imbedded in the sand or mud, which sometimes preserves their harder parts from decay, and sometimes keeps only their impress. The remains of the animals and plants of the land may also be washed out to sea; but these will more often be found in lakes and in river-beds. On the other hand, rocks exposed to the air will receive little fresh material, and will gradually be worn away and carried out to sea, the softer rocks yielding the sooner. Any organic relics which they may contain will be destroyed by the action of wind and weather, or removed far from their original home. Roughly speaking, then, we may say that times of deposition have been times of submergence. Such submergence has never been general. Depression in one part involves elevation in another. Earth movements are constantly in progress, and they are usually slow and imperceptible, often amounting only to a few inches in a century. Violent convulsions are the exception, not the rule; and, though small islands may occasionally be born of volcanic action, the great continents are produced by gradual folding of the earth-crust. Thus the greater part of the Scandinavian peninsula, at the present time, is slowly rising. Deep-sea corals, killed by being carried up into shallower and warmer waters, have been found in Christiania fiord; and the pines on the edges of the Norwegian snow-fields are dying from the increased cold consequent on elevation. In Cornwall, and on both sides of Scotland, old sea beaches are found at various distances inland. These are proofs of upheaval, while depression is proved by the remains of submerged forests, and by those long, narrow inlets of the sea called fiords, which terminate inland in glens, and are nothing else than submerged river-valleys.

When Europe lay under deep sea, in Silurian times, a great continent stretched north and south through the middle of what is now the Atlantic Ocean. What was the life of this continent we cannot tell; we can scarcely even guess its general character, as the most westerly part of Europe now elevated must have lain too far to the east to receive any organic *débris* from the shores. Yet there can be no doubt that abundant life was nourished on the dry land of this "buried Atlantis," as well as in the deep ocean of our present dwelling-place. Again, there is a great biological chasm between the red sandstones which cover the coal and those immediately overlying them. The beds are similar in colour and texture; but the fossils in the lower seem like memories of an old *régime*—those in the upper like promises of a new. Does this great gulf signify that life was absent? Is it the record of a secular night, when no fresh forms came into being, and when the generating forces of Nature were dormant? No, we cannot question that the process of evolution was unbroken in this time, as in others; but, owing to the elevation and denudation of the land, no remains have been preserved. The new types which appear in the Trias did not start into life with the dawn of a new day; they were the children of lost species, of whose existence we may be confident, although they died and left no sign.

What, then, is the conclusion of the whole matter? It is this: The earth's history is a mutilated book, with far more gaps than pages. Here whole sheets are gone; there the very half-page is torn out which might have explained the whole. But what is left gives evidence that the narrative was continuous, and that rough handling, not disconnected writing, is answerable for its present fragmentary condition. The conception of a "geological period" is a mere fiction, convenient for purposes of retention and classification, but not expressing any actual truth. The time of greatest change and most vigorous vitality in any special region may often be unrepresented in its strata; and the higher vertebrates, from their terrestrial habits, will generally be more scantily preserved than lower forms. Our chronology rests chiefly on molluscan remains ; and, could the evolutionary history of some higher forms of life be taken as the standard, the "periods" might present a very different aspect; but in no case should we find any mornings and evenings, any night, or any time of Sabbatic rest. The line of Nature is an ascending spiral, in which we can trace no beginning and can foresee no end—a succession of curves, interrupted by no angle. Constant activity, ceaseless play of Protean forces, is now, and ever has been, the law of life.

Charlotte Perkins Gilman

Similar Cases

CHARLOTTE PERKINS GILMAN (1860-1935) *is nowadays best known for her short horror story "The Yellow Wall-Paper" (1892), although her output was immense. An innovative writer on the American feminist scene whose legacy has been damaged by her embrace of eugenics, Gilman was a fervent political analyst and satirist. "Similar Cases," published under her short-lived married surname, Stetson, scathingly employs the lessons of evolutionary theory against contemporary social conservatism. Appearing in the monthly socialist magazine,* The Nationalist, *in April 1890, the poem is jocularly dedicated to various economists. The gradual evolution from small creatures like* Eohippus *into the modern horse was typically considered an outstanding example of progress and improvement in the natural world.*[1]

I.

There was once a little animal, no bigger than a fox.
And on five toes he scampered over Tertiary rocks.
They called him Eohippus, and they called him very small,
And they thought him of no value when they thought of him at all.
For the lumpish Dinoceras and Coryphodont so slow
Were the heavy aristocracy in days of long ago.
Said the little Eohippus: "I am going to be a Horse!
And on my middle-finger-nails to run my earthly course!
I'm going to have a flowing tail! I'm going to have a mane!

1 Stephen Jay Gould, "Life's Little Joke," *Natural History*, 94 (1988), 16-25.

I'm going to stand fourteen hands high on the Psychozoic plain!"
The Coryphodont was horrified, the Dinoceras shocked;
And they chased young Eohippus, but he skipped away and mocked.
Then they laughed enormous laughter, and they groaned enormous groans,
And they bade young Eohippus "go and view his father's bones!"
Said they: "You always were as low and small as now we see,
And therefore it is evident you're always going to be!
What! Be a great, tall, handsome beast with hoofs to gallop on!
Why, you'd have to change your nature!" said the Loxolophodon.
Then they fancied him disposed of, and retired with gait serene;
That was the way they argued in 'the Early Eocene.'

II.

There was once an Anthropoidal Ape, far smarter than the rest,
And everything that they could do he always did the best;
So they naturally disliked him, and they gave him shoulders cool,
And, when they had to mention him, they said he was a fool.
Cried this pretentious ape one day: "I'm going to be a Man!
And stand upright, and hunt and fight, and conquer all I can!
I'm going to cut down forest trees to make my houses higher!
I'm going to kill the Mastodon! I'm going to make a Fire!"
Loud screamed the Anthropoidal Apes with laughter wild and gay;
Then tried to catch that boastful one, but he always got away.
So they yelled at him in chorus, which he minded not a whit;
And they pelted him with cocoanuts, which didn't seem to hit.
And then they gave him reasons which they thought of much avail
To prove how his preposterous attempt was sure to fail.
Said the sages: "In the first place, the thing can *not* be done!
And second, if it *could* be, it would not be any fun!
And third and most conclusive, and admitting no reply,
You would have to change your nature! We should like to see you try!"
They chuckled then triumphantly, those lean and hairy shapes;

For these things passed as arguments—with the Anthropoidal Apes!

III.

There was once a Neolithic Man, an enterprising wight,
Who made his simple implements unusually bright.
Unusually clever he, unusually brave,
And he sketched delightful mammoths on the borders of his cave.
To his Neolithic neighbors, who were startled and surprised,
Said he: "My friends, in course of time, we shall be civilized!
We are going to live in Cities and build churches and make laws!
We are going to eat three times a day without the natural cause!
We're going to turn life upside-down about a thing called Gold!
We're going to want the earth and take as much as we can hold!
We're going to wear a pile of stuff outside our proper skins;
We are going to have Diseases! and Accomplishments!! and Sins!!!"
Then they all rose up in fury against their boastful friend;
For prehistoric patience comes quickly to an end.
Said one: "This is chimerical! Utopian! Absurd!"
Said another: "What a stupid life! Too dull, upon my word!"
Cried all: "Before such things can come, you idiotic child,
You must alter Human Nature!" and they all sat back and smiled.
Thought they: 'An answer to that last it will be hard to find!'
It was a clinching argument—to the Neolithic Mind!

Phil Robinson

The Last of the Vampires

During the Victorian fin de siècle *disturbing stories about survivals from prehistory became familiar items in the fiction sections of popular periodicals. These stories unnervingly turned conceptions of evolutionary progress on their head and brought humans up against eerie creatures previously thought extinct.* PHIL ROBINSON (1847-1902) *was an Anglo-Indian journalist and litterateur who travelled all over the world, known especially for his cheerful writings on natural history.* "The Last of the Vampires," *published in the* Contemporary Review *in March 1893, begins urbanely enough, but quickly gives way to a dark, hallucinatory tale of scientific obsession.*

Do you remember the discovery of the "man-lizard" bones in a cave on the Amazon some time in the forties? Perhaps not. But it created a great stir at the time in the scientific world and, in a lazy sort of way, interested men and women of fashion. For a day or two it was quite the correct thing for Belgravia to talk of "connecting links," of "the evolution of man from the reptile," and "the reasonableness of the ancient myths" that spoke of Centaurs and Mermaids as actual existences.

The fact was that a German Jew, an india-rubber merchant, working his way with the usual mob of natives through a cahucho forest along the Marañon, came upon some bones on the river-bank where he had pitched his camp. Idle curiosity made him try to put them together, when he found, to his surprise, that he had before him the skeleton of a creature with human

85

legs and feet, a dog-like head and immense bat-like wings.
Being a shrewd man, he saw the possibility of money being
made out of such a curiosity; so he put all the bones he could
find into a sack and, on the back of a llama, they were in due
course conveyed to Chachapoyas, and thence to Germany.

Unfortunately, his name happened to be the same as that of
another German Jew who had just then been trying to hoax the
scientific world with some papyrus rolls of a date anterior to
the Flood, and who had been found out and put to shame. So
when his namesake appeared with the bones of a winged man,
he was treated with very scant ceremony.

However, he sold his india-rubber very satisfactorily, and as
for the bones, he left them with a young medical student of
the ancient University of Bierundwurst, and went back to his
cahucho trees and his natives and the banks of the Amazon.
And there was an end of him.

The young student one day put his fragments together, and,
do what he would, could only make one thing of them—a
winged man with a dog's head.

There were a few ribs too many, and some odds and ends
of backbone which were superfluous; but what else could be
expected of the anatomy of so extraordinary a creature? From
one student to another the facts got about, and at last the professors came to hear of it; and, to cut a long story short, the
student's skeleton was taken to pieces by the learned heads of
the college, and put together again by their own learned hands.

But do what they would, they would only make one thing
of it—a winged man with a dog's head.

The matter became serious: the professors were at first puzzled, and then got quarrelsome; and the results of their squab-
bling was that pamphlets and counterblasts were published;
and so all the world got to hear of the bitter controversy about
the "man-lizard of the Amazon."

One side declared, of course, that such a creature was an

impossibility, and that the bones were a remarkably clever hoax. The other side retorted by challenging the sceptics to manufacture a duplicate, and publishing the promise of such large rewards to any one who would succeed in doing so, that the museum was beset for months by competitors. But no one could manufacture another man-lizard. The man part was simple enough, provided they could get a human skeleton. But at the angles of the wings were set huge claws, black, polished, and curved, and nothing that ingenuity could suggest would imitate them. And then the "Genuinists," as those who believed in the monster called themselves, set the "Imposturists" another poser; for they publicly challenged them to say what animal either the head or the wings had belonged to, if not to the man-lizard? And the answer was never given.

So victory remained with them, but not, alas! the bones of contention. For the Imposturists, by bribery and burglary, got access to the precious skeleton, and lo! one morning the glory of the museum had disappeared. The man half of it was left, but the head and wings were gone, and from that day to this no one has ever seen them again.

And which of the two factions was right? As a matter of fact, neither; as the following fragments of narrative will go to prove.

Once upon a time, so say the Zaporo Indians, who inhabit the district between the Amazon and the Marañón, there came across to Pampas de Sacramendo a company of gold-seekers, white men, who drove the natives from their workings and took possession of them. They were the first white men who had ever been seen there, and the Indians were afraid of their guns; but eventually treachery did the work of courage, for, pretending to be friendly, the natives sent their women among the strangers, and they taught them how to make tucupi out of the bread-root, but they did not tell them how to distinguish between the ripe and the unripe. So the wretched white men made tucupi out of the unripe fruit (which brings on fits like epilepsy) and when they were lying about the camp, helpless, the Indians attacked them and killed them all.

All except three. These three they gave to the Vampire.

But what was the Vampire? The Zaporos did not know. "Very long ago," said they, "there were many vampires in Peru, but they were all swallowed up in the year of the Great Earthquake when the Andes were lifted up, and there was left behind only one 'Arinchi,' who lived where the Amazon joins the Marañon, and he would not eat dead bodies—only live ones, from which the blood would flow."

So far the legend; and that it had some foundation in fact is proved by the records of the district, which tell of more than one massacre of white gold-seekers on the Marañon by Indians whom they had attempted to oust from the washings; but of the Arinchi, the Vampire, there is no official mention. Here, however, other local superstitions help us to the reading of the riddle of the man-lizard of the University at Bierundwurst.

When sacrifice was made to "the Vampire," the victim was bound in a canoe, and taken down the river to a point where there was a kind of winding back-water, which had shelving banks of slimy mud, and at the end there was a rock with a cave in it. And here the canoe was left. A very slow current flowed through the tortuous creek, and anything thrown into the water ultimately reached the cave. Some of the Indians had watched the canoes drifting along, a few yards only in an hour, and turning round and round as they drifted, and had seen them reach the cave and disappear within. And it had been a wonder to them, generation after generation, that the cave was never filled up, for all day long the current was flowing into it, carrying with it the sluggish flotsam of the river. So they said that the cave was the entrance to Hell, and bottomless.

And one day a white man, a professor of that same University of Bierundwurst, and a mighty hunter of beetles before the Lord, who lived with the Indians in friendship, went up the backwater, right up to the entrance, and set afloat inside the cave a little raft, heaped up with touch-wood and knots of the oil-tree, which he set fire to, and he saw the raft go creeping along, all ablaze, for an hour and more, lighting up the wet walls of the cave as it went on either side; and then *it was put out.*

It did not "go" out suddenly, as it if had upset, or had floated over the edge of a waterfall, but just as if it had been beaten out.

For the burning fragments were flung to one side and the other, and the pieces, still alight, glowed for a long time on the ledges and points of rock where they fell, and the cave was filled with the sound of a sudden wind and the echoes of the noise of great wings flapping.

And at last, one day, this professor went into the cave himself.

"I took," he wrote, "a large canoe, and from the bows I built out a brazier of stout cask-hoops, and behind it set a gold-washing tin dish for a reflector, and loaded the canoe with roots of the resin-tree, and oil-wood, and yams, and dried meat; and I took spears with me, some tipped with the woorali poison, that numbs but does not kill. And so I drifted inside the cave; and I lit my fire, and with my pole I guided the canoe very cautiously through the tunnel, and before long it widened out, and creeping along one wall I suddenly became aware of a moving of something on the opposite side.

"So I turned the light fair upon it, and there, upon a kind of ledge, sate a beast with a head like a large grey dog. Its eyes were as large as a cow's.

"What its shape was I could not see. But as I looked I began gradually to make out two huge bat-like wings, and these were spread out to their utmost as if the beast were on tiptoe and ready to fly. And so it was. For just as I had realised that I beheld before me some great bat-reptile of a kind unknown to science, except as prediluvian, and the shock had thrilled through me at the thought that I was actually in the presence of a living specimen of the so-called extinct flying lizards of the Flood, the thing launched itself upon the air, and the next instant it was upon me.

"Clutching on to the canoe, it beat with its wings at the flame so furiously that it was all I could do to keep the canoe from capsizing, and, taken by surprise, I was nearly stunned by the strength and rapidity of its blows before I attempted to defend myself.

"By that time—scarcely half a minute had elapsed—the brazier had been emptied by the powerful brute; and the vampire, mistaking me no doubt for a victim of sacrifice, had already taken hold of me. The next instant I had driven a spear clean through its body, and with a prodigious tumult of wings, the thing loosed its claws from my clothes and dropped off into the stream.

"As quickly as possible I rekindled my light, and now saw the Arinchi, with wings outstretched upon the water, drifting down on the current. I followed it.

"Hour after hour, with my reflector turned full upon that grey dog's head with cow-like eyes, I passed along down the dark and silent waterway. I ate and drank as I went along, but did not dare to sleep. A day must have passed, and two nights; and then, as of course I had all along expected, I saw right ahead a pale eye-shaped glimmer, and knew that I was coming out into daylight again.

"The opening came nearer and nearer, and it was with intense eagerness that I gazed upon the trophy, the floating Arinchi, the last of the Winged Reptiles.

"Already in imagination I saw myself the foremost of travellers in European fame—the hero of my day. What were Banks' kangaroos or De Chaillu's gorilla to my discovery of the last survivor of the pterodactyles, of the creatures of Flood—the flying Saurian of the pre-Noachian epoch of catastrophe and mud?

"Full of these thoughts, I had not noticed that the vampire was no longer moving, and suddenly the bow of the canoe bumped against it. In an instant it had climbed up on to the boat. Its great bat-like wings once more beat me and scattered the flaming brands, and the thing made a desperate effort to get past me back into the gloom. It had seen the daylight approaching and rather than face the sun, preferred to fight.

"Its ferocity was that of a maddened dog, but I kept it off with my pole, and seeing my opportunity as it clung, flapping its wings, upon the bow, gave it such a thrust as made it drop off. It began to swim (I then for the first time noticed its long neck), but with my pole I struck it on the head and stunned it, and once more saw it go drifting on the current into daylight.

"What a relief it was to be out in the open air! It was noon, and as we passed out from under the entrance of the cave, the river blazed so in the sunlight that after the two days of almost total darkness I was blinded for a time. I turned my canoe to the shore, to the shade of trees, and throwing a noose over the floating body, let it tow behind.

"Once more on firm land—and in possession of the Vampire!

"I dragged it out of the water. What a hideous beast it looked, this winged kangaroo with a python's neck! It was not dead; so I made a muzzle with a strip of skin, and then I firmly bound its wings together round its body. I lay down and slept. When I awoke, the next day was breaking; so, having breakfasted, I dragged my captive into the canoe and went on down the river. Where I was I had no idea; but I knew that I was going to the sea: going to Germany: and that was enough.

★　★　★　★　★

"For two months I have been drifting with the current down this never-ending river. Of my adventures, of hostile natives, of rapids, of alligators, and jaguars, I need say nothing. They are the common property of all travellers. But my vampire! It is alive. And now I am devoured by only one ambition—to keep it alive, to let Europe actually gaze upon the living, breathing, survivor of the great Reptiles known to the human race before the days of Noah—the missing link between the reptile and the bird. To this end I denied myself food; denied myself even precious medicine. In spite of itself I gave it all my quinine, and when the miasma crept up the river at night, I covered it with my rug and lay exposed myself. If the black fever should seize me!

* * * * *

"Three months, and still upon this hateful river! Will it never end? I have been ill—so ill, that for two days I could not feed it. I had not the strength to go ashore to find food, and I fear that it will die—die before I can get it home.

* * * * *

"Been ill again—the black fever! But *it* is alive. I caught a vicuna swimming in the river, and it sucked it dry—gallons of blood. It had been unfed three days. In its hungry haste it broke its muzzle. I was almost too feeble to put it on again. A horrible thought possesses me. Suppose it breaks its muzzle again when I am lying ill, delirious, and it is ravenous? Oh! the horror of it! To see it eating is terrible. It links the claws of its wings together, and cowers over the body; its head is under the wings, out of sight. But the victim never moves. As soon as the vampire touches it there seems to be a paralysis. Once those wings are linked there is an absolute quiet. Only the grating of teeth upon bone. Horrible! horrible! But in Germany I shall be famous. *In Germany with my Vampire?*

★ ★ ★ ★ ★

"Am very feeble. It broke its muzzle again. But it was in the daylight—when it is blind. Its great eyes are blind in sunlight. It was a long struggle. This black fever! and the horror of this thing! I am too weak now to kill it, if I would. I *must* get it home alive. Soon—surely soon—the river will end. Oh God! does it never reach the sea, reach white men, reach home? But if it attacks me I will throttle it. If I am dying I will throttle it. If we cannot go back to Germany alive, we will go together dead. I will throttle it with my two hands, and fix my teeth in its horrible neck, and our bones shall lie together on the bank of this accursed river."

★ ★ ★ ★ ★

This is nearly all that was recovered of the professor's diary. But it is enough to tell us of the final tragedy.

The two skeletons *were* found together on the very edge of the river-bank. Half of each, in the lapse of years, had been washed away at successive flood-tides. The rest, when put together, made up the man-reptile that, to use a Rabelaisian phrase, "metagrobolised all to nothing" the University of Bierundwurst.

C. J. Cutcliffe Hyne
(writing as Weatherby Chesney)

The Crimson Beast

The fiction of C. J. CUTCLIFFE HYNE *(1865–1944), writing here under the name Weatherby Chesney, was highly profitable during the 1890s and early twentieth century. An English author adept at tapping into and fueling widespread fascination with empire, conquest, and globetrotting, Hyne was most famous as the creator of the roguish Captain Kettle, for a time one of the few literary characters who could rival the popularity of Sherlock Holmes. His fiction frequently dealt with science and technology, including paleontology. This particular tale of prehistoric subterranean peril appeared in Hyne's unpromisingly titled collection* The Adventures of a Solicitor *(1898), ostensibly a novel but in effect a series of breezy and only loosely connected short stories. An alternative and rather different version of the story, entitled "The Lizard," appeared in the* Strand Magazine *during the same year.*

IT makes me smile sometimes grimly to myself when I hear people thanking their stars that we have no wild beasts in this snug England of ours to make the woods unsafe, or to devour the children from before the cottage door. And I smile, too, when men and women with a smattering of geology point to some fossilized bones, and speak of the greater of this earth's animals as being habitants of a prehistoric age, and thoroughly extinct for many a weary thousand years.

But with my smile comes a shudder, for when fate brought me in contact with the last beast of a species which our scientists of to-day say was rare when Adam first used his spade, fate at the same time let me rub shoulders with old Death in one of his most terrifying forms.

It was my weakness for rambling which led me into the plight. An office stool is an abomination to me, but a necessity, since it is ordained that I should earn my bread (together with the necessary modicum of luxury) as a solicitor. But the fresh air draws me, and the moorlands of our north country are my delight.

I had gone up to the hills on that day with a friend to watch the grouse rearing their young, and for hours we gazed with interest at the wild, brown birds as they led their fluffy chicks amongst the clumps of heather, and taught them the two great lessons of hiding from the sight of man, and finding food to give strength to their limbs and bodies.

We were walking some twenty yards apart, and had wandered over the rough moorland almost to the other side. Below us were the rocks and stone walls of the hill flank, and below again, the rich water-meadows of the valley. And it was at that point that Chadwick sang out, "Hullo, Dale! come here and look."

I went across, and found him lying on his belly at the mouth of a hole.

"It is newly fallen in," he cried. "Look at the sides. By Jove! we may find a way down there into a new cave."

I shared his excitement, for I also had learnt the fascination of cave-hunting in this limestone district. But when he suggested clambering down there and then, I demurred.

"No," I said, "that's only inviting a broken neck. The passage twists at twenty feet down, as you can see for yourself. And listen!" I picked up a boulder and threw it. "There, you see, the drop is considerable."

"Right you are," said Chadwick. "I don't hanker after attending my own funeral just yet. There's a farm down there on the hillside, not a mile away. I'll go and get a cart rope and some candles;" and he scrambled to his feet.

"I'll go with you," I said; and together we set off down the slopes, talking eagerly enough of what we were going to find.

We came back with a great coil of the rope which the farmer used to make fast hay-loads on the shelvins of his carts, a bunch of tallow candles (lead-miners' candles they were, really), and a heavy iron crowbar.

We drove the crowbar into the ground, slantingwise, almost to its head, made fast the rope in a bowline knot, and threw the slack end of it down into the hole. Then we tossed for first descent, and Chadwick won.

He was soon out of sight, carrying with him an avalanche of dirt and pebbles, and presently I heard his voice, muffled and small, come up from below.

"Dale! All right. Easy going. Only mind don't trundle down any more stones than you can help, or they'll hit you on the head."

"Mind your own skull below, then!" I shouted.

"Oh, I'm under shelter," he bawled back. "Come on."

I took hold of the rope, and let it slip through my hands. It was worn very smooth with use. I quickly reached the point where the hole turned, and the light above me dimmed, and a patter of earth rained on me. The rope swung with my weight like a pendulum, and I should say the sheer descent was a matter of forty feet. But at that distance I splashed into water, and lowered myself more gently till I found bottom. It covered me to the knees. I saw the yellow glow of Chadwick's candle further on in the darkness.

As I fumbled for my own matches and lit up, he explained matters to me excitedly.

"Dale, old man," he cried, "we've stumbled on a great discovery. This promises to be one of the biggest caves I've seen. Who knows but what we may strike a vein of lead in it and make our fortunes?"

Lead-mining supplies the excitement for our Yorkshire dales, not gold.

"Is it all wet?"

"There's water behind you, and deep. I've been in it up to my neck. However, the roof comes down in that direction, and one can't get any further there. But come along to me: I'm on dry land here."

I stumbled towards him over a floor of slippery boulders, and presently stepped out of the water and stood on hard, dry mud. We lit all our candles, and held them up together. We were in one of the most enormous caverns I have ever seen. The roof was not distinguishable through the gloom. The sides were eighty feet apart, and the length we had yet to explore. Left stranded by a fall of the water in a hollow of the mud at my feet lay a dead fish.

"Look there!" I said.

Chadwick picked it up. "Eyeless," he said, "like all the fish in mine-water and these cave lakes. By Jove! I shall come down here and see if these fellows will swallow a worm on a hook."

"All right," said I; "another day for that; but for the present let's explore further."

"Right you are," said he; and we set off together, with new expressions of wonder at every step. Never in all Yorkshire and Derbyshire was there such another cave as this discovery of ours, we told ourselves; and we were right, though we did not know the reason then.

But gradually our exultation began to lessen. The cave walls drew nearer to one another; the roof drooped; the further end seemed to be approaching. And then we came to a pond of black water which seemed to bar all further progress.

"There's a beach on the further side," said Chadwick. "Look, you can see it gleam when I hold up the light. I am going to swim across, and try if I can't get further."

"Very well," said I; "we neither of us can be much wetter

than we are already. So here goes to come with you."

We each picked up a lump of clay, fastened the candles, miner-fashion, to our hats, and dropped into the water. The chill of it struck me to the bone and slowed my movements. Moreover, I am never at any time a rapid swimmer. Chadwick shot quickly ahead of me, and I saw him haul himself on to the ledge of rock. And then such a glow of horror seized me that I nearly sank. A great swirl stirred the water behind my heels. Something rose beneath me and scraped swiftly past my chest. And my hands struck on a cold, live body that shuddered under the touch.

How I got out I do not know; I think Chadwick must have helped me; for the next thing I remember was standing beside him on that narrow ledge, and seeing his face next mine, white as paper in the candle-glow.

"So you saw it too?" I gasped.

"Who could help seeing it?" he replied. "And look at your hands, man!"

I looked. They were all smothered in slime like an eel's, only this slime was crimson, and it smelt of musk, not fish.

"Good God!" I cried, "what was it? Am I really awake, or is this some abominable dream?"

The answer came of itself. Once more the beast rose from the black depths of the pool with a great swirl of the water, and then sank; and presently it appeared again, floating half-submerged on the surface, and lying there quietly, as though listening. It had the head of a crocodile, with teeth sticking out at the side of its jaws like those on a saw-fish's snout; its body was as big as a cow's, only twice as long, and tapering off into a tail like an otter's; and on each of its flanks it had a pair of limbs, half leg, half fin, something like a turtle's. The body was covered with a smooth, scaleless skin, crimson in colour, and covered with gouts of slime.

"Prehistoric survival," said Chadwick, trying to be cool, though his teeth were rattling. "That thing ought to have been extinct a thousand centuries ago, by all the laws of textbooks. Old man, we are in a mess."

I fully agreed with him, but I did not say so aloud. The creature had apparently heard his voice, and was turning itself with its paddles so as to head directly towards us. Then it began to swim slowly forward, and the full loathsomeness showed plain in the candlelight. It was absolutely without eyes; there were not even so much as sockets where eyes once had been in its ancestors. It opened its huge jaws and showed a palate sown with teeth. The little blind fish we had noted before formed its food. I saw the remains of one sticking to a fringing tooth.

We stood as still as death, and the beast swam towards us, lifting its snout in the air, and apparently trying to scent us. I saw its nostrils working in and out, but I think its power of smell must have been small, for presently it gave up those tactics and tried another.

It lifted its head on to the ledge of rock where we stood, and then laboriously brought up a huge, slimy fore-flapper. It was going to grope for us, and seize us where we stood.

Instinctively, we both turned to run, then for the first time realized to the full our horrible situation. The narrow ledge of rock on which we stood was the end of the cave. There was no further passage. We were in a *cul de sac*.

I felt the beast's breath cold and clammy upon my ankles, and the instinct of the hunted mended my wit. I had in my pocket a penknife—a miserable, dainty thing with a tortoise-shell handle, barely heavy enough to sharpen a pencil. With fumbling fingers I pulled it out and opened the blade. The beast was nuzzling for me with its quick-moving head. I raised my hand and stabbed at the crimson flesh with repeated blows.

The blade tore great scores in the beast's head, but it made no cry. It was horribly dumb. But it followed me with a hound's persistence, champing its thousand teeth, and slobbering on the rock. I was covered to the elbows with the horrible crimson slime. And gradually I was being cornered. In spite of my blows, the beast with its clumsy crawl was driving me before it towards the unyielding wall of rock.

In another yard my retreat must have come to an end, and then those awful teeth would close on my limbs, and I almost froze with terror at the thought. But in the nick of time Chadwick made a diversion in my favour. He also had a weapon, a heavy clasp-knife, but for a full minute his numbed fingers refused to open the blade. At last, however, it gleamed open in the light, and he raised it and stabbed. The creature's rear was towards him, and he drove his blade in where the tail is joined to the body.

The effect was marvellous. To my slashing at its head the beast had paid no heed; at this other attack, it turned with its clumsy movements and hissed like some monstrous cat. It made for Chadwick open-jawed, and he sprang back, crying for help. I made good use of my new knowledge.

So soon as ever the vulnerable spot came within my reach, I buried the penknife in it halfway up the tortoiseshell handle.

Again the huge, blind beast swerved round hissing, and the battle raged between the three of us till the place was crimson with slime, and we two humans panted with the violence of our stabbings.

But at last the beast gave in. It wallowed on its flappers to the edge of the rock, and toppled over into the black water, and sank slowly out of sight. A few bubbles came up to show where it had gone. And that was all.

"Now," cried Chadwick, "in with you, Dale, before it comes back;" and freezing with terror, we plunged in also, and swam across with desperate strokes to the opposite side. But we were undisturbed, and though we stood there for many an hour in that musky atmosphere, watching the surface of that black pool till all our candles were expended, its surface was not again disturbed.

We climbed back to the moor then, and went home, saying nothing of what we had seen. And on the following days, and, in fact, at intervals for many weeks, we returned to that cave with arms and fishing material, in hopes that we might lure the beast into capture, and so acquire fame in showing it. But never a glimpse or a sign of the beast did we ever get again. The alligator smell of musk had cleared from the air; and in the end, when we gave up the quest, we were ashamed to speak of what we had seen, lest listeners, after their custom when they hear of anything strange which cannot be produced in evidence, should openly scoff, and call us liars for our tale.

But at the same time we advertised to no one the finding of the new cave, lest some unfortunate wight should go there and die a horrible death through the beast coming once more to the surface. For, mind you, although we injured that hateful, blind, scarlet creature to the utmost of our ability, both Chadwick and myself are firmly convinced that we did not kill it. If its enormous vitality had helped it to endure through all those eras of time since its fellows disappeared from the surface of the earth, it was not likely to succumb to the attacks of our puny weapons.

Wardon Allan Curtis

The Monster of Lake LaMetrie

The American author WARDON ALLAN CURTIS (1867-1940) *possessed a distinctly weird imagination, as demonstrated by this unique story, published in the transatlantic* Pearson's Magazine *in September 1899. Taking place in Wyoming, "The Monster of Lake LaMetrie" tells of another scientific expedition that goes horribly wrong after a surviving relic of prehistory is discovered. The setting is precise: during the year of the story's publication, Wyoming was hounded by employees of East Coast natural history museums racing to excavate giant dinosaur fossils (although the titular "Monster" is not actually a dinosaur).[1] Curtis melds Wyoming's prehistoric associations with a classic conspiracy theory that had been promoted by the army officer John Cleves Symmes Jr. back in 1818. According to Symmes, the earth is hollow and the interior can be accessed via holes at the poles.[2] Curtis appropriates this evocative device, but his mind-bending short story brings even stranger events to bear on its unfortunate protagonists.*

1 Paul D. Brinkman, *The Second Jurassic Dinosaur Rush: Museums and Paleontology in America at the Turn of the Twentieth Century* (Chicago: University of Chicago Press, 2010).
2 Conway Zirkle, "The Theory of Concentric Spheres: Edmund Halley, Cotton Mather, & John Cleves Symmes," *Isis*, 37 (1947), 155-159.

Being the narration of James McLennegan, M.D., Ph.D.

LAKE LAMETRIE, WYOMING,
APRIL 1st, 1899.

Prof. William G. Breyfogle,
University of Taychobera.

DEAR FRIEND,—Inclosed you will find some portions of the diary it has been my life-long custom to keep, arranged in such a manner as to narrate connectedly the history of some remarkable occurrences that have taken place here during the last three years. Years and years ago, I heard vague accounts of a strange lake high up in an almost inaccessible part of the mountains of Wyoming. Various incredible tales were related of it, such as that it was inhabited by creatures which elsewhere on the globe are found only as fossils of a long vanished time.

The lake and its surroundings are of volcanic origin, and not the least strange thing about the lake is that it is subject to periodic disturbances, which take the form of a mighty boiling in the centre, as if a tremendous artesian well were rushing up there from the bowels of the earth. The lake rises for a time, almost filling the basin of black rocks in which it rests, and then recedes, leaving on the shores mollusks and trunks of strange trees and bits of strange ferns which no longer grow—on the earth, at least—and are to be seen elsewhere only in coal measures and beds of stone. And he who casts hook and line into the dusky waters, may haul forth ganoid fishes completely covered with bony plates.

All of this is described in the account written by Father LaMetrie years ago, and he there advances the theory that the earth is hollow, and that its interior is inhabited by the forms of plant and animal life which disappeared from its surface ages ago, and that the lake connects with this interior region. Symmes' theory of polar orifices is well known to you. It is amply corroborated. I know that it is true now. Through the great holes at the poles, the sun sends light and heat into the interior.

Three years ago this month, I found my way through the mountains here to Lake LaMetrie accompanied by a single companion, our friend, young Edward Framingham. He was led to go with me not so much by scientific fervor, as by a faint hope that his health might be improved by a sojourn in the mountains, for he suffered from an acute form of dyspepsia that at times drove him frantic.

Beneath an overhanging scarp of the wall of rock surrounding the lake, we found a rudely-built stone house left by the old cliff dwellers. Though somewhat draughty, it would keep out the infrequent rains of the region, and serve well enough as a shelter for the short time which we intended to stay.

The extracts from my diary follow:

APRIL 29TH, 1896.

I have been occupied during the past few days in gathering specimens of the various plants which are cast upon the shore by the waves of this remarkable lake. Framingham does nothing but fish, and claims that he has discovered the place where the lake communicates with the interior of the earth, if, indeed, it does, and there seems to be little doubt of that. While fishing at a point near the centre of the lake, he let down three pickerel lines tied together, in all nearly three hundred feet, without finding bottom. Coming ashore, he collected every bit of line, string, strap, and rope in our possession, and made a line five hundred feet long, and still he was unable to find the bottom.

MAY 2ND, EVENING.

The past three days have been profitably spent in securing specimens, and mounting and pickling them for preservation.

Framingham has had a bad attack of dyspepsia this morning and is not very well. Change of climate had a brief effect for the better upon his malady, but seems to have exhausted its force much sooner than one would have expected, and he lies on his couch of dry water-weeds, moaning piteously. I shall take him back to civilisation as soon as he is able to be moved.

It is very annoying to have to leave when I have scarcely begun to probe the mysteries of the place. I wish Framingham had not come with me. The lake is roaring wildly without, which is strange, as it has been perfectly calm hitherto, and still more strange because I can neither feel nor hear the rushing of the wind, though perhaps that is because it is blowing from the south, and we are protected from it by the cliff. But in that case there ought to be no waves on this shore. The roaring seems to grow louder momentarily. Framingham—

MAY 3RD, MORNING.

Such a night of terror we have been through. Last evening, as I sat writing in my diary, I heard a sudden hiss, and, looking down, saw wriggling across the earthen floor what I at first took to be a serpent of some kind, and then discovered was a stream of water which, coming in contact with the fire, had caused the startling hiss. In a moment, other streams had darted in, and before I had collected my senses enough to move, the water was two inches deep everywhere and steadily rising.

Now I knew the cause of the roaring, and, rousing Framingham, I half dragged him, half carried him to the door, and digging our feet into the chinks of the wall of the house, we climbed up to its top. There was nothing else to do, for above us and behind us was the unscalable cliff, and on each side the ground sloped away rapidly, and it would have been impossible to reach the high ground at the entrance to the basin.

After a time we lighted matches, for with all this commotion there was little air stirring, and we could see the water, now half-way up the side of the house, rushing to the west with the force and velocity of the current of a mighty river, and every little while it hurled tree-trunks against the house-walls with a terrific shock that threatened to batter them down. After an hour or so, the roaring began to decrease, and finally there was an absolute silence. The water, which reached to within a foot of where we sat, was at rest, neither rising nor falling.

Presently a faint whispering began and became a stertorous breathing, and then a rushing like that of the wind and a roaring rapidly increasing in volume, and the lake was in motion again, but this time the water and its swirling freight of tree-trunks flowed by the house toward the east, and was constantly falling, and out in the centre of the lake the beams of the moon were darkly reflected by the sides of a huge whirlpool, streaking the surface of polished blackness down, down, down the vortex into the beginning of whose terrible depths we looked from our high perch.

This morning the lake is back at its usual level. Our mules are drowned, our boat destroyed, our food damaged, my specimens and some of my instruments injured, and Framingham is very ill. We shall have to depart soon, although I dislike exceedingly to do so, as the disturbance of last night, which is clearly like the one described by Father LaMetrie, has undoubtedly brought up from the bowels of the earth some strange and interesting things. Indeed, out in the middle of the lake where the whirlpool subsided, I can see a large quantity of floating things; logs and branches, most of them probably, but who knows what else?

Through my glass I can see a tree-trunk, or rather stump, of enormous dimensions. From its width I judge that the whole tree must have been as large as some of the Californian big trees. The main part of it appears to be about ten feet wide and thirty feet long. Projecting from it and lying prone on the water is a limb, or root, some fifteen feet long, and perhaps two or three feet thick. Before we leave, which will be as soon as Framingham is able to go, I shall make a raft and visit the mass of driftwood, unless the wind providentially sends it ashore.

MAY 4TH, EVENING.

A day of most remarkable and wonderful occurrences. When I arose this morning and looked through my glass, I saw that the mass of driftwood still lay in the middle of the lake, motionless on the glassy surface, but the great black stump had disappeared. I was sure it was not hidden by the rest of the drift-wood, for yesterday it lay some distance from the other logs, and there had been no disturbance of wind or water to change its position. I therefore concluded that it was some heavy wood that needed to become but slightly waterlogged to cause it to sink.

Framingham having fallen asleep at about ten, I sallied forth to look along the shores for specimens, carrying with me a botanical can, and a South American machete, which I have possessed since a visit to Brazil three years ago, where I learned the usefulness of this sabre-like thing. The shore was strewn with bits of strange plants and shells, and I was stooping to pick one up, when suddenly I felt my clothes plucked, and heard a snap behind me, and turning about I saw—but I won't describe it until I tell what I did, for I did not fairly see the terrible creature until I had swung my machete round and sliced off the top of its head, and then tumbled down into the shallow water where I lay almost fainting.

Here was the black log I had seen in the middle of the lake, a monstrous elasmosaurus, and high above me on the heap of rocks lay the thing's head with its long jaws crowded with sabre-like teeth, and its enormous eyes as big as saucers. I wondered that it did not move, for I expected a series of convulsions, but no sound of a commotion was heard from the creature's body, which lay out of my sight on the other side of the rocks.

I decided that my sudden cut had acted like a stunning blow and produced a sort of coma, and fearing lest the beast should recover the use of its muscles before death fully took place, and in its agony roll away into the deep water where I could not secure it, I hastily removed the brain entirely, performing the operation neatly, though with some trepidation, and restoring to the head the detached segment cut off by my machete, I proceeded to examine my prize.

In length of body, it is exactly twenty-eight feet. In the widest part it is eight feet through laterally, and is some six feet through from back to belly. Four great flippers, rudimentary arms and feet, and an immensely long, sinuous, swan-like neck, complete the creature's body. Its head is very small for the size of the body and is very round and a pair of long jaws project in front much like a duck's bill. Its skin is a leathery integument of a lustrous black, and its eyes are enormous hazel optics with a soft, melancholy stare in their liquid depths. It is an elasmosaurus, one of the largest of antediluvian animals. Whether of the same species as those whose bones have been discovered, I cannot say.

My examination finished, I hastened after Framingham, for I was certain that this waif from a long past age would arouse almost any invalid. I found him somewhat recovered from his attack of the morning, and he eagerly accompanied me to the elasmosaurus. In examining the animal afresh, I was astonished to find that its heart was still beating and that all the functions of the body except thought were being performed one hour after the thing had received its death blow, but I knew that the hearts of sharks have been known to beat hours after being removed from the body, and that decapitated frogs live, and have all the powers of motion, for weeks after their heads have been cut off.

I removed the top of the head to look into it and here another surprise awaited me, for the edges of the wound were granulating and preparing to heal. The colour of the interior of the skull was perfectly healthy and natural, there was no undue flow of blood, and there was every evidence that the animal intended to get well and live without a brain. Looking at the interior of the skull, I was struck by its resemblance to a human skull; in fact, it is, as nearly as I can judge, the size and shape of the brain-pan of an ordinary man who wears a seven and an eighth hat. Examining the brain itself, I found it to be the size of an ordinary human brain, and singularly like it in general contour, though it is very inferior in fibre and has few convolutions.

MAY 5TH, MORNING.

Framingham is exceedingly ill and talks of dying, declaring that if a natural death does not put an end to his sufferings, he will commit suicide. I do not know what to do. All my attempts to encourage him are of no avail, and the few medicines I have no longer fit his case at all.

MAY 5TH, EVENING.

I have just buried Framingham's body in the sand of the lake shore. I performed no ceremonies over the grave, for perhaps the real Framingham is not dead, though such a speculation seems utterly wild. To-morrow I shall erect a cairn upon the mound, unless indeed there are signs that my experiment is successful, though it is foolish to hope that it will be.

At ten this morning, Framingham's qualms left him, and he set forth with me to see the elasmosaurus. The creature lay in the place where we left it yesterday, its position unaltered, still breathing, all the bodily functions performing themselves. The wound in its head had healed a great deal during the night, and I daresay will be completely healed within a week or so, such is the rapidity with which these reptilian organisms repair damages to themselves. Collecting three or four bushels of mussels, I shelled them and poured them down the elasmosaurus's throat. With a convulsive gasp, they passed down and the great mouth slowly closed.

"How long do you expect to keep the reptile alive?" asked Framingham.

"Until I have gotten word to a number of scientific friends, and they have come here to examine it. I shall take you to the nearest settlement and write letters from there. Returning, I shall feed the elasmosaurus regularly until my friends come, and we decide what final disposition to make of it. We shall probably stuff it."

"But you will have trouble in killing it, unless you hack it to pieces, and that won't do. Oh, if I only had the vitality of that animal. There is a monster whose vitality is so splendid that the removal of its brain does not disturb it. I should feel very happy if someone would remove my body. If I only had some of that beast's useless strength."

"In your case, the possession of a too active brain has injured the body," said I. "Too much brain exercise and too little bodily exercise are the causes of your trouble. It would be a pleasant thing if you had the robust health of the elasmosaurus, but what a wonderful thing it would be if that mighty engine had your intelligence."

I turned away to examine the reptile's wounds, for I had brought my surgical instruments with me, and intended to dress them. I was interrupted by a burst of groans from Framingham and turning, beheld him rolling on the sand in an agony. I hastened to him, but before I could reach him, he seized my case of instruments, and taking the largest and sharpest knife, cut his throat from ear to ear.

"Framingham, Framingham," I shouted and, to my astonishment, he looked at me intelligently. I recalled the case of the French doctor who, for some minutes after being guillotined, answered his friends by winking.

"If you hear me, wink," I cried. The right eye closed and opened with a snap. Ah, here the body was dead and the brain lived. I glanced at the elasmosaurus. Its mouth, half closed over its gleaming teeth, seemed to smile an invitation. The intelligence of the man and the strength of the beast. The living body and the living brain. The curious resemblance of the reptile's brain-pan to that of a man flashed across my mind.

"Are you still alive, Framingham?"

The right eye winked. I seized my machete, for there was no time for delicate instruments. I might destroy all by haste and roughness, I was sure to destroy all by delay. I opened the skull and disclosed the brain. I had not injured it, and breaking the wound of the elasmosaurus's head, placed the brain within. I dressed the wound and, hurrying to the house, brought all my store of stimulants and administered them.

For years the medical fraternity has been predicting that brain-grafting will some time be successfully accomplished. Why has it never been successfully accomplished? Because it has not been tried. Obviously, a brain from a dead body cannot be used and what living man would submit to the horrible process of having his head opened, and portions of his brain taken for the use of others?

The brains of men are frequently examined when injured and parts of the brain removed, but parts of the brains of other men have never been substituted for the parts removed. No uninjured man has ever been found who would give any portion of his brain for the use of another. Until criminals under sentence of death are handed over to science for experimentation, we shall not know what can be done in the way of brain-grafting. But public opinion would never allow it.

Conditions are favourable for a fair and thorough trial of my experiment. The weather is cool and even, and the wound in the head of the elasmosaurus has every chance for healing. The animal possesses a vitality superior to any of our later day animals, and if any organism can successfully become the host of a foreign brain, nourishing and cherishing it, the elasmosaurus with its abundant vital forces can do it. It may be that a new era in the history of the world will begin here.

MAY 6TH, NOON.

I think I will allow my experiment a little more time.

MAY 7TH, NOON.

It cannot be imagination. I am sure that as I looked into the elasmosaurus's eyes this morning there was expression in them. Dim, it is true, a sort of mistiness that floats over them like the reflection of passing clouds.

MAY 8TH, NOON.

I am more sure than yesterday that there *is* expression in the eyes, a look of troubled fear, such as is seen in the eyes of those who dream nightmares with unclosed lids.

MAY 11TH, EVENING.

I have been ill, and have not seen the elasmosaurus for three days, but I shall be better able to judge the progress of the experiment by remaining away a period of some duration.

MAY 12TH, NOON.

I am overcome with awe as I realise the success that has so far crowned my experiment. As I approached the elasmosaurus this morning, I noticed a faint disturbance in the water near its flippers. I cautiously investigated, expecting to discover some fishes nibbling at the helpless monster, and saw that the commotion was not due to fishes, but to the flippers themselves, which were feebly moving.

"Framingham, Framingham," I bawled at the top of my voice. The vast bulk stirred a little, a very little, but enough to notice. Is the brain, or Framingham, it would perhaps be better to say, asleep, or has he failed to establish connection with the body? Undoubtedly he has not yet established connection with the body, and this of itself would be equivalent to sleep, to unconsciousness. As a man born with none of the senses would be unconscious of himself, so Framingham, just beginning to establish connections with his new body, is only dimly conscious of himself and sleeps. I fed him, or it—which is the proper designation will be decided in a few days—with the usual allowance.

MAY 17TH, EVENING.

I have been ill for the past three days, and have not been out of doors until this morning. The elasmosaurus was still motionless when I arrived at the cove this morning. Dead, I thought; but I soon detected signs of breathing, and I began to prepare some mussels for it, and was intent upon my task, when I heard a slight, gasping sound, and looked up. A feeling of terror seized me. It was as if in response to some doubting incantations there had appeared the half-desired, yet wholly-feared and unexpected apparition of a fiend. I shrieked, I screamed, and the amphitheatre of rocks echoed and re-echoed my cries, and all the time the head of the elasmosaurus raised aloft to the full height of its neck, swayed about unsteadily, and its mouth silently struggled and twisted, as if in an attempt to form words, while its eyes looked at me now with wild fear and now with piteous intreaty.

"Framingham," I said.

The monster's mouth closed instantly, and it looked at me attentively, pathetically so, as a dog might look.

"Do you understand me?"

The mouth began struggling again, and little gasps and moans issued forth.

"If you understand me, lay your head on the rock."

Down came the head. He understood me. My experiment was a success. I sat for a moment in silence, meditating upon the wonderful affair, striving to realise that I was awake and sane, and then began in a calm manner to relate to my friend what had taken place since his attempted suicide.

"You are at present something in the condition of a partial paralytic, I should judge," said I, as I concluded my account. "Your mind has not yet learned to command your new body. I see you can move your head and neck, though with difficulty. Move your body if you can. Ah, you cannot, as I thought. But it will all come in time. Whether you will ever be able to talk or not, I cannot say, but I think so, however. And now if you cannot, we will arrange some means of communication. Anyhow, you are rid of your human body and possessed of the powerful vital apparatus you so much envied its former owner. When you gain control of yourself, I wish you to find the communication between this lake and the under-world, and conduct some explorations. Just think of the additions to geological knowledge you can make. I will write an account of your discovery, and the names of Framingham and McLennegan will be among those of the greatest geologists."

I waved my hands in my enthusiasm, and the great eyes of my friend glowed with a kindred fire.

JUNE 2ND, NIGHT.

The process by which Framingham has passed from his first powerlessness to his present ability to speak, and command the use of his corporeal frame, has been so gradual that there has been nothing to note down from day to day. He seems to have all the command over his vast bulk that its former owner had, and in addition speaks and sings. He is singing now. The north wind has risen with the fall of night, and out there in the darkness I hear the mighty organ pipe-tones of his tremendous, magnificent voice, chanting the solemn notes of the Gregorian, the full throated Latin words mingling with the roaring of the wind in a wild and weird harmony.

To-day he attempted to find the connection between the lake and the interior of the earth, but the great well that sinks down in the centre of the lake is choked with rocks and he has discovered nothing. He is tormented by the fear that I will leave him, and that he will perish of loneliness. But I shall not leave him. I feel too much pity for the loneliness he would endure, and besides, I wish to be on the spot should another of those mysterious convulsions open the connection between the lake and the lower world.

He is beset with the idea that should other men discover him, he may be captured and exhibited in a circus or museum, and declares that he will fight for his liberty even to the extent of taking the lives of those attempting to capture him. As a wild animal, he is the property of whomsoever captures him, though perhaps I can set up a title to him on the ground of having tamed him.

JULY 6.

One of Framingham's fears has been realised. I was at the pass leading into the basin, watching the clouds grow heavy and pendulous with their load of rain, when I saw a butter-fly net appear over a knoll in the pass, followed by its bearer, a small man, unmistakably a scientist, but I did not note him well, for as he looked down into the valley, suddenly there burst forth with all the power and volume of a steam calliope, the tremendous voice of Framingham, singing a Greek song of Anacreon to the tune of "Where did you get that hat?" and the singer appeared in a little cove, the black column of his great neck raised aloft, his jagged jaws wide open.

That poor little scientist. He stood transfixed, his butterfly net dropped from his hand, and as Framingham ceased his singing, curvetted and leaped from the water and came down with a splash that set the whole cove swashing, and laughed a guffaw that echoed among the cliffs like the laughing of a dozen demons, he turned and sped through the pass at all speed.

I skip all entries for nearly a year. They are unimportant.

JUNE 30TH, 1897.

A change is certainly coming over my friend. I began to see it some time ago, but refused to believe it and set it down to imagination. A catastrophe threatens, the absorption of the human intellect by the brute body. There are precedents for believing it possible. The human body has more influence over the mind than the mind has over the body. The invalid, delicate Framingham with refined mind, is no more. In his stead is a roistering monster, whose boisterous and commonplace conversation betrays a constantly growing coarseness of mind.

No longer is he interested in my scientific investigations, but pronounces them all bosh. No longer is his conversation such as an educated man can enjoy, but slangy and diffuse iterations concerning the trivial happenings of our uneventful life. Where will it end? In the absorption of the human mind by the brute body? In the final triumph of matter over mind and the degradation of the most mundane force and the extinction of the celestial spark? Then, indeed, will Edward Framingham be dead, and over the grave of his human body can I fittingly erect a headstone, and then will my vigil in this valley be over.

FORT D. A. RUSSELL, WYOMING,

APRIL 15TH, 1899.

Prof. William G. Breyfogle.

DEAR SIR,—The inclosed intact manuscript and the fragments which accompany it, came into my possession in the manner I am about to relate and I inclose them to you, for whom they were intended by their late author. Two weeks ago, I was dispatched into the mountains after some Indians who had left their reservation, having under my command a company of infantry and two squads of cavalrymen with mountain howitzers. On the seventh day of our pursuit, which led us into a wild and unknown part of the mountains, we were startled at hearing from somewhere in front of us a succession of bellowings of a very unusual nature, mingled with the cries of a human being apparently in the last extremity, and rushing over a rise before us, we looked down upon a lake and saw a colossal, indescribable thing engaged in rending the body of a man.

Observing us, it stretched its jaws and laughed, and in saying this, I wish to be taken literally. Part of my command cried out that it was the devil, and turned and ran. But I rallied them, and thoroughly enraged at what we had witnessed, we marched down to the shore, and I ordered the howitzers to be trained upon the murderous creature. While we were doing this, the thing kept up a constant blabbing that bore a distinct resemblance to human speech, sounding very much like the jabbering of an imbecile, or a drunken man trying to talk. I gave the command to fire and to fire again, and the beast tore out into the lake in its death-agony, and sank.

With the remains of Dr. McLennegan, I found the foregoing manuscript intact, and the torn fragments of the diary from which it was compiled, together with other papers on scientific subjects, all of which I forward. I think some attempt should be made to secure the body of the elasmosaurus. It would be a priceless addition to any museum.

Arthur W. Fairchild,

Captain U.S.A.

Reginald Bacchus and Cyril Ranger Gull

The Dragon of St. Paul's

*Spectacular fossil discoveries and even rumors of the genuine survival of large prehistoric creatures fed what was called the "new journalism," a phenomenon that came to the fore in the late-nineteenth century. This sensational and populist form of reportage, developed by authors and editors in the United States and Britain, frequently narrowed and exploited the ambiguous proximity of fact and fiction.[1] This short story about the intrusion of a prehistoric reptile into contemporary London begins with a group of consciously modern and cynical journalists whose laxity with the truth is exploded when reality turns out to be stranger than fiction. Among other things, *REGINALD BACCHUS (1874-1945) *was a writer of erotic literature, while his co-author* CYRIL RANGER GULL *(1875-1923), under a variety of pseudonyms, penned lurid mystery novels. "The Dragon of St. Paul's" appeared in the April 1899 edition of the* Ludgate Monthly, *a magazine whose title refers to Ludgate Hill, the location of St. Paul's Cathedral, where the London "Dragon" makes its last stand.*

IN THREE EPISODES.

FIRST EPISODE.

"IT is certainly a wonderful yarn," said Trant, "and excellent

---

1 For key studies, see Karen Roggenkamp, *Narrating the News: New Journalism and Literary Genre in Late Nineteenth-Century American Newspapers and Fiction* (Kent, Ohio: Kent State University, 2005); and Joel H. Wiener, *The Americanization of the British Press, 1830s-1914: Speed in the Age of Transatlantic Journalism* (Basingstoke: Palgrave Macmillan, 2011).

copy. My only regret is that I didn't think of it myself in the first instance."

"But, Tom, why shouldn't it be true? It's incredible enough for any one to believe. I'm sure I believe it, don't you, Guy?"

Guy Descaves laughed. "Perhaps, dear. I don't know and I don't much care, but I did a good little leaderette on it this morning. Have you done anything, Tom?"

"I did a whole buck middle an hour ago at very short notice. That's why I'm a little late. I had finished all my work for the night, and I was just washing my hands when Fleming came in with the make-up. We didn't expect him at all to-night, and the paper certainly was rather dull. He'd been dining somewhere, and I think he was a little bit cocked. Anyhow he was nasty, and kept the presses back while I did a 'special' on some information he brought with him."

While he was talking, Beatrice Descaves, his *fiancée*, began to lay the table for supper, and in a minute she called them to sit down. The room was very large, with cool white-papered walls, and the pictures, chiefly original black and white sketches, were all framed in *passe-partout* frames, which gave the place an air of serene but welcome simplicity. At one end of it was a great window which came almost to the floor, and in front of the window there was a low, cushioned seat. The night was very hot, and the window was wide open. It was late— nearly half-past one, and London was quite silent. Indeed the only sound that they could hear was an occasional faint burst of song and the tinkling of a piano, which seemed to come from the neighbourhood of Fountain Court.

Guy Descaves was a writer, and he lived with his sister Beatrice in the Temple. Trant, who was also a journalist on the staff of a daily paper, and who was soon going to marry Beatrice, often came to them there after his work was done. The three young people lived very much together, and were very happy in a delightful unfettered way. The Temple was quiet and close to their work, and they found it in these summer days a most peaceful place when night had come to the town.

They were very gay at supper in the big, cool room. Trant was a clever young man and very much in love, and the presence of Beatrice always inspired him to talk. It was wonderful to sit by her, and to watch her radiant face, or to listen to the music of her laugh which rippled like water falling into water. Guy, who was more than thirty, and was sure that he was very old, liked to watch his sister and his friend together, and to call them "you children."

"What is the special information that the editor brought, dear?" Beatrice asked Trant, as soon as they were seated round the table.

"Well," he answered. "It seems that he managed to get hold of young Egerton Cotton, Professor Glazebrook's assistant, who is staying at the Metropole. Of course various rumours have got about from the crew of the ship, but nothing will be definitely known till the inquest to-morrow. Cotton's story is really too absurd, but Fleming insisted on its going in."

"Did he give him much for his information?" Descaves asked.

"Pretty stiff, I think. I know the *Courier* offered fifty, but he stuck out. Fleming only got it just at the last moment. It's silly nonsense, of course, but it'll send the sales up to-morrow."

"What is the whole thing exactly?" Beatrice asked. "All that I've heard is that Professor Glazebrook brought back some enormous bird from the Arctics, and that just off the Nore the thing escaped and killed him. I'm sure that sounds quite sufficiently extraordinary for anything; but I suppose it's all a lie."

"Well," said Trant. "What Egerton Cotton says is the most extraordinary thing I have ever heard—it's simply laughable— but it will sell three hundred thousand extra copies. I'll tell you. I've got the whole thing fresh in my brain. You know that Professor Glazebrook was one of the biggest biologists who have ever lived, and he's been doing a great, tedious, monumental book on prehistoric animals, the mammoth and all that sort of thing that E. T. Reed draws in *Punch*. Some old scientific Johnny in Wales used to find all the money, and he fitted out the Professor's exploration ship, the "Henry Sandys," to go and find these mammoths and beasts which have got frozen up in the ice. Don't you remember about two years ago when they started from Tilbury? They got the Lord Mayor down, and a whole host of celebrities, to see them go. I was there reporting, I remember it well, and Reggie Lance did an awfully funny article about it, which he called 'The hunting of the Snark.' Well, Egerton Cotton tells Fleming—the man *must* be mad—that they found a whole lot of queer bears and things frozen up, but no very great find until well on into the second year, when they were turning to come back. Fleming says he's seen all the diaries and photographs and everything; they had a frightfully hard time. At last one day they came across a great block of ice, and inside it, looking as natural as you please, was a huge winged sort of dragon creature, as big as a cart horse. Fleming saw a photograph. I don't know how they faked it up, and he says it was the most horrid cruel sort of thing you ever dreamt of after lobster salad. It had big, heavy wings, and a beak like a parrot, little flabby paws all down its body like a caterpillar, and a great bare, pink, wrinkled belly. Oh, the most filthy-looking brute! They cut down the ice till it was some decent size, and they hauled the whole thing chock-a-block, like a prune in a jelly, into the hold. The ice was frightfully hard, and one of the chains of the donkey engine broke once, and the whole thing fell, but even then the block held firm. It took them three weeks to get it on board. Well, they sailed away with their beastly Snark as jolly as sandboys, and Cotton says the Professor was nearly out of his mind with joy—used to talk and mumble to himself all day. They put the thing in a huge refrigerator like the ones the Australian mutton comes over in, and Glazebrook used to turn on the electric lights and sit muffled up in furs watching his precious beast for hours."

He stopped for a moment to light a cigarette, noticing with amusement that Guy and Beatrice were becoming tremendously interested. He made Beatrice pour him out a great tankard of beer before he would go on, and he moved to the window-seat, where it was cooler, and he could sit just outside the brilliant circle of light thrown by the tall shaded lamp. The other two listened motionless, and as he unfolded the grisly story, his voice coming to them out of the darkness became infinitely more dramatic and impressive.

"Well, Cotton says that this went on for a long time. He had to do all the scientific work himself, writing up their journals and developing the photos, as the Professor was always mysteriously pottering about in the cellar place. At last, one day, Glazebrook came into the cabin at lunch or whatever they have, and said he was going to make a big experiment. He talked a lot of rot about toads and reptiles being imprisoned for thousands of years in stones and ice, and then coming to life, and he said he was going to try and melt out the dragon and tickle it into life with a swingeing current from the dynamo. Cotton laughed at him, but it wasn't any good, and they set to work to thaw the creature out with braziers. When they got close to it Cotton said that the water from the ice, as it melted, got quite brown and *smelt!* It wasn't till they were within almost a few hours from the Channel—you remember they put into some place in Norway for coal—and steaming for London River as hard as they could go, that they got it clear.

"While they were fixing the wires from the dynamo room, Cotton hurt his ankle and had to go to his bunk for some hours to rest. He begged Glazebrook to wait till he could help, for he had become insensibly interested in the whole uncanny thing, but it was no use. He says the fellow was like a madman, red eyes with wrinkles forming up all round them, and so excited that he was almost foaming at the mouth. He went to his cabin frightfully tired, and very soon fell asleep. One of the men woke him up by shaking him. The man was in a blue funk and told him something dreadful had happened in the hold. Cotton hobbled up to the big hatchway, which was open, and as he came near it with the mate and several of the men, he said he could hear a coughing choked-up kind of noise, and that there was a stench like ten thousand monkey houses. They looked in and saw this great beast *alive!* and squatting over Glazebrook's body picking out his inside like a bird with a dead crab."

Beatrice jumped up with a scream. "Oh Tom, Tom, don't, you horrid boy! I won't hear another word. I shan't sleep a wink. Ugh! how disgusting and ridiculous. Do you mean to tell me that you've actually gone to press with all that ghastly nonsense? I'm going to bathe my face, you've made me feel quite hot and sticky. You can tell the rest to Guy, and if you haven't done by the time I come back, I won't say good-night to you, there!"

She left the room, not a little disconcerted by the loathsome story which Trant, forgetting his listeners, had been telling with the true journalist's passion for sensational detail. Guy knocked the ashes slowly out of his pipe. "Well?" he said.

"Oh, there isn't much more. He says they all ran away and watched from the companion steps, and presently the beast came flopping up on deck, with its beak all over blood, and its neck coughing and working. It got half across the hatchway and seemed dazed for about an hour. No one seemed to think of shooting it! Then Cotton says it crawled to the bulwarks coughing and grunting away, and after a few attempts actually flew up into the air. He said it flew unlike any creature he had ever seen, much higher than most birds fly, and very swiftly. The last they saw of it was a little thing like a crow hovering over the forts at Shoe'ness."

"Well, I'm damned," said Guy. "I never heard a better piece

of yarning in my life. Do you mean to tell me that Fleming dares to print all that gaudy nonsense in the paper. He must certainly have been very drunk."

"Well, there it is, old man. I had to do what I was told, and I made a good piece of copy out of it. I am not responsible if Fleming does get his head laughed off, I don't edit his rag. Pass the beer."

"Is the ship here?"

"Yes, it was docked about six this morning, and so far all the published news is what you had to-day in the *Evening Post*. It seems that something strange certainly did happen, though of course it wasn't that. They are going to hold an inquest, Fleming says. Something horribly beastly has happened to Glazebrook, there's no doubt of that. Something has scooped the poor beggar out. Well, I must be going, it's nearly three, and more than a little towards dawning. Tell Bee I'm off, will you?"

Beatrice came back in a minute like a fresh rose, and before he went she drew him on to the balcony outside the window. There was a wonderful view from the balcony. Looking over the great lawns far down below, they could just see the dim purple dome of St. Paul's which seemed to be floating in mist, its upper part stark and black against the sky. To the right was the silent river with innumerable patches of yellow light from the rows of gas lamps on Blackfriars bridge. A sweet scent from the boxes of mignonette floated on the dusky, heavy air. He put his arm round her and kissed her sweet, tremulous lips. "My love, my love," she whispered, "oh, I love you so!"

Her slender body clung to him. She was very sweet. The tall, strong young man leant over her and kissed her masses of dark, fragrant hair.

"My little girl, my little girl," he murmured with a wonderful tenderness in his voice, "there is nothing in the world but you, sweet little girl, dear, dear little girl, little wife."

She looked up at him at the word and there was a great light in her eyes, a thing inexpressibly beautiful for a man to see.

"Love, good-night," he whispered, and he kissed the tiny pink ear that heard him.

After the fantastic story he had been telling them, a story which, wild and grotesque as it was, had yet sufficient *vraisemblance* to make them feel uncomfortable, the majesty of the night gave the dim buildings of the town a restful and soothing effect, and as they stood on the balcony with their love surging over them, they forgot everything but that one glorious and radiant fact.

Beatrice went with him to the head of the staircase—they lived very high up in the buildings called "Temple Gardens"—and watched him as he descended. It was curious to look down the great well of the stone steps and to feel the hot air which rose up from the gas lamps beating on her face. She could only see Tom on each landing when he turned to look up at her—a tiny pink face perched on a little black fore-shortened body.

When he got right down to the bottom he shouted up a "good night," his voice sounding strange and unnatural as the walls threw it back to each other. In after years she always remembered the haunting sound of his voice as it came to her for the last time in this world.

Between seven and eight o'clock the next morning Guy, who was on the staff of the *Evening Post*, one of the leading lunch-time papers, left the Temple for the offices in the Strand.

It was a beautiful day, and early as it was the streets were full of people going to their work. Even now the streets were full of colour and sunshine, and every little city clerk contributed to the gayness of the scene by wearing round his straw hat the bright ribbon of some club to which he did not belong.

Guy had been working for about an hour when Gobion, his assistant—the young man who afterwards made such a success with his book "Penny Inventions,"—came in with a bunch of "flimsies," reports of events sent in by penny-a-liners who scoured London on bicycles, hoping for crime.

"There doesn't seem anything much," he said, "except one thing which is probably a fake. It was brought in by that man, Roberts, and he tried to borrow half a James from the commissionaire on the strength of it, which certainly looks like a fake. If it is true, though, it's good stuff. I've sent a reporter down to inquire."

"What is it?" said Descaves, yawning.

"Reported murder of a journalist. The flimsy says he was found at four o'clock in the morning by a policeman, on the steps of St. Paul's absolutely broken up and mangled. Ah, here it is. '*The body, which presented a most extraordinary and unaccountable appearance, was at once removed to St. Bride's mortuary.*' Further details later, Roberts says."

"It sounds all right; at any rate the reporter will be back soon, and we shall know. How did Roberts spot him as a journalist?"

"Don't know, suppose he hadn't shaved."

While the youth was speaking, the reporter entered breathless.

"Column special," he gasped. "Trant, a man on the *Mercury*, has been murdered, cut all to pieces. Good God! I forgot, Descaves. Oh, I am fearfully sorry!"

Guy rose quickly from his seat with a very white face, but without any sound. As he did so by some strange coincidence the tape machine on the little pedestal behind him began to print the first words of a despatch from the Exchange Telegraph Company. The message dealt with the tragedy that had taken immediate power of speech away from him. The familiar whirr of the type wheel made him turn from mere force of habit, and stunned as his brain was, he saw the dreadful words spelling themselves on the paper with no realisation of their meaning. He stood swaying backwards and forwards, not knowing what he did, his eyes still resting on the broad sheet of white paper on which the little wheel sped ceaselessly, recording the dreadful thing in neat blue letters.

Then suddenly his eyes flashed the meaning of the gathering words to his brain, and he leant over the glass with a sick eagerness. Gobion and the reporter stood together anxiously watching him. At length the wheel slid along the bar and came to rest with a sharp click. Guy stood up again.

"Do my work to-day," he said quietly. "I must go to my sister," and taking his hat he left the room.

When he got out into the brilliant sunshine which flooded the Strand, his senses came back to him and he determined that obviously the first thing to be done was to make sure that the body at St. Bride's was really the body of his friend.

Even in moments of deep horror and sorrow the mind of a strong, self-contained man does not entirely lose its power of concentration. The Telegraphic news had left very little doubt in his mind that the fact was true, but at the same time he could not conceive how such a ghastly thing could possibly have happened. According to the information he had, it seemed the poor fellow had been struck dead only a few minutes after he had left the Temple the night before, and within a few yards of his chambers. "On the steps of St. Paul's" the wire ran, and Trant's rooms were not sixty yards away, in a little old-fashioned court behind the Deanery.

It was incredible. Owing to the great shops and warehouses all round, the neighbourhood was patrolled by a large number of policemen and watchmen. The space at the top of Ludgate Hill was, he knew, brilliantly lighted by the street lamps, and besides, about four it was almost daylight. It seemed impossible that Tom could have been done to death like this. "It's a canard," he said to himself, "damned silly nonsense," but even as he tried to trick himself into disbelief, his sub-conscious brain told him unerringly that the horrid thing was true.

Five minutes later he walked out of the dead house knowing

the worst. The horror of the thing he had just seen, the awful inexpressible horror of it, killed every other sensation. He had recognised his friend's right hand, for on the hand was a curious old ring of beaten gold which Beatrice used to wear.

SECOND EPISODE.

Mr. Frank Fleming, the editor of the *Daily Mercury*, was usually an early riser. He never stopped at the office of the paper very late unless some important news was expected, or unless he had heard something in the House that he wished to write about himself. Now and then, however, when there was an all-night sitting, he would steal away from his bench below the gangway and pay a surprise visit before Trant and his colleagues had put the paper to bed. On these occasions, when he was kept away from his couch longer than was his wont, he always slept late into the morning. It was about twelve o'clock on the day of Trant's death that he rose up in bed and pressed the bell for his servant. The man brought his shaving water and the morning's copy of the *Mercury*, and retired. Fleming opened his paper and the black headline and leaded type of the article on Professor Glazebrook's death at once caught his eye. He read it with complacent satisfaction. Trant had done the thing very cleverly and the article was certainly most striking. Fleming, a shrewd man of the world and Parliamentary adventurer, had not for a moment dreamt of believing young Egerton Cotton, but he nevertheless knew his business. It had got about that there was something mysterious in the events that had occurred on board the "Henry Sandys," and it had also got about that the one man who could throw any authentic light on these events was Cotton. It was therefore the obvious policy to buy Cotton's information, and, while disclaiming any responsibility for his statements, to steal a march on his contemporaries by being the first to publish them. As he walked into the pretty little dining-room of his flat, Mr. Fleming was in an excellent temper.

He was dividing his attention between the kidneys and the *Times*, when his man came into the room and told him that Mr. Morgan, the news editor, must see him immediately.

He could hear Morgan in the *entresol*, and he called out cheerily, "Come in, Morgan; come in, you're just in time for some breakfast."

The news editor entered in a very agitated state. When Fleming heard the undoubted fact of Trant's death he was genuinely moved, and Morgan, who had a very low opinion of his chief's human impulses, was surprised and pleased. It seemed that Morgan had neither seen the body nor been to the scene of the crime, but had simply got his news from some men in the bar of the "Cheshire Cheese," in Fleet Street, who were discussing the event. Trant had been a very popular man among his brethren, and many men were mourning for him as they went about their work.

"What you must do," said Fleming to his assistant, "is this. Go down to the mortuary on my behalf, explain who Trant was, and gain every morsel of information you can. Go to the place where the body was found as well. Poor Tom Trant! He was a nice boy—a nice boy; he had a career before him. I shall walk down to the office. This has shaken me very much, and I think a walk will buck me up a little. If you get a fast cab and tell the man to go Hell for Leather, you will be back in Fleet Street by the time I arrive. I shall not walk fast." He heaved a perfectly sincere sigh as he put on his gloves. As he left the mansions and walked past the Aquarium he remembered that a cigar was a soothing thing, and, lighting one, he enjoyed it to the full. The sunshine was so radiant that it was indeed difficult to withstand its influence. Palace Yard was a great sight, and all the gilding on the clock tower shone merrily. The pigeons, with their strange iridescent eyes, were sunning themselves on the hot stones. The editor forgot all about Trant for some minutes in the pure physical exhilaration of it all. As he advanced up Parliament Street he saw Lord Salisbury, who was wearing an overcoat, despite the heat.

Fleming turned up Whitehall Court and past the National Liberal Club to the Strand, which was very full of people. Fleming had always been a great patron of the stage. He knew, and was known to, many actors and actresses, and you would always see his name after a ten-guinea subscription on a benefit list. He liked the Strand, and he walked very slowly down the north side, nodding or speaking to some theatrical acquaintance every moment.

When he came to the bar where all the actors go, which is nearly opposite the Tivoli Music Hall, he saw Rustle Tapper, the famous comedian, standing on the steps wearing a new white hat and surveying the bright and animated scene with intense enjoyment.

The two men were friends, and for a minute or two Fleming mounted the steps and stood by the other's side. It was now about half-past one.

"Well," said the actor, "and how are politics, very busy just now? What is this I see in the *Pall Mall* about the murder of one of your young men? It's not true, I hope."

"I am afraid it is only too true. He was the cleverest young fellow I have ever had on the paper. I got him straight from Baliol, and he would have been a very distinguished man. I don't know anything about it yet but just the bare facts; our news editor has gone down to find out all he can."

They moved through the swing doors into the bar, talking as they went.

The Strand was full of all its regular frequenters, and in the peculiar fashion of this street every one seemed to know every one else intimately. Little groups of more or less well-known actors and journalists stood about the pavement or went noisily in and out of the bars, much impeding the progress of the ordinary passer-by. There was no sign or trace of anything out of the common to be seen. It was just the Strand on a bright summer's day, and the flower-girls were selling all their roses very fast to the pretty burlesque actresses and chorus girls who were going to and fro from the agents' offices.

About two o'clock—the evening papers said half-past two, but their information was faulty—the people in Bedford Street and the Strand heard a great noise of shouting, which, as far as they could judge, came from the direction of the Haymarket or Trafalgar Square. The noise sounded as if a crowd of people were shouting together, but whether in alarm or whether at the passing of some great person was not immediately apparent.

It was obvious that something of importance was happening not very far away. After about a minute the shouting became very loud indeed, and a shrill note of alarm was plainly discernible. In a few seconds the pavements were crowded with men, who came running out from the bars and restaurants to see what was happening. Many of them came out without their hats. Fleming and the actor hurried out with the rest, straining and pushing to get a clear view westwards. One tall, clean-shaven man, with a black patch on his eye, his face bearing obvious traces of grease paint, came out of the Bun Shop with his glass of brandy and water still in his hand.

It was a curious sight. Everyone was looking towards Trafalgar Square with mingled interest and uncertainty, and for the time all the business of the street was entirely suspended. The drivers of the omnibuses evidently thought that the shouting came from fire-engines which were trying to force their way eastwards through the traffic, for they drew up by the curbstone, momentarily expecting that the glistening helmets would swing round the corner of King William Street.

Fleming, from the raised platform at the door of Gatti's, could see right down past Charing Cross station, and as he was nearly six feet high, he could look well over the heads of the podgy little comedians who surrounded him. Suddenly the noise grew in volume and rose several notes higher, and a black mass of people appeared running towards them.

The next incident happened so rapidly that before any one had time for realisation it was over. A huge black shadow sped along the dusty road, and, looking up, the terror-stricken crowd saw the incredible sight of a vast winged creature, as large as a dray-horse, gliding slowly over the street. The monster, which Fleming describes as something like an enormous bat with a curved bill like a bird of prey, began to hover, as if preparing to descend, when there was the sudden report of a gun. An assistant at the hosier's shop at the corner of Southampton Street, who belonged to the Volunteers, happened to be going to do some range firing in the afternoon, and fetching his rifle from behind the counter, took a pot shot at the thing. His aim, from surprise and fear, was bad, and the bullet only chipped a piece of stone from the coping of the Tivoli. The shot, however, made the creature change its intentions, for it swerved suddenly to the right against some telegraph wires, and then, breaking through them, flew with extraordinary swiftness away over the river, making, it appeared, for the Crystal Palace upon Sydenham Hill. A constable on Hungerford foot-bridge, who saw it as it went over the water, said that its hairless belly was all cut and bleeding from the impact of the wires. The excitement in the Strand became frantic. The windows of all the shops round the Tivoli were broken by the pressure of the crowd, who had instinctively got as near as possible to the houses. The cab and omnibus horses, scenting the thing, were in that state of extreme terror which generally only an elephant has power to induce in them. The whole street was in terrible confusion. The only person who seemed calm, so a report ran in a smart evening paper, was a tall man who was standing at the door of a bar wearing a patch over one eye,

and who had a glass of brandy in his hand. A reporter who had
been near him, said that as soon as the monster had disappeared
over the house-tops, he quietly finished his glass of brandy, and
straightway went inside to have it replenished.

Special editions of the evening papers were at once issued.
The *Globe*, owning to the nearness of its offices, being first in
the field.

The sensational story of the *Mercury*, which had been the
signal for increasing laughter all the morning, came at once
into men's minds, and, incredible as it was, there could now be
no doubt of the truth.

A creature which, in those dim ages when the world was
young and humanity itself was slowly being evolved in obedience to an inevitable law, had winged its way over the mighty
swamps and forests of the primeval world, was alive and prey-
ing among them. To those who thought, there was something
sinister in such an incalculable age. The order of nature was
disturbed.

The death of young Trant was immediately explained, and
at dinner time the wildest rumours were going about the clubs,
while in the theatres and music-halls people were saying that a
whole foul brood of dragons had been let loose upon the town.

The sensation was unique. Never before in all the history of
the world had such a thing been heard of, and all night long
the telegraphs sent conflicting rumours to the great centres of
the earth. London was beside itself with excitement, and few
people going about in the streets that night felt over secure,
though everyone felt that the slaughter of the beast was only
a matter of hours. The very uneasiness that such a weird and
unnatural appearance excited in the brains of the populace had
its humorous side, and when that evening Mr. Dan Leno chose
to appear upon the stage as a comic St. George, the laughter was
Homeric. Such was the state of the public opinion about the
affair on the evening of the first day, but there was a good deal

of anxiety felt at Scotland Yard, and Sir Edward Bradford was for some time at work organising and directing precautionary measures. A company of sharp-shooters was sent down to the Embankment from the Regent's Park Barrack, and waited in readiness for any news. Mounted police armed with carbines were patrolling the whole country round Sydenham, and even as far as Mitcham Common were on the alert. Two or three of them rode constantly up and down the Golf Links.

A warning wire was despatched to Mr. Henry Gillman, the general manager of the Crystal Palace, for at this season of the year the grounds were always full of pleasure-seekers. About nine o'clock the chief inspector on duty at the police headquarters received the following telegram.

"Animal appeared here 8.30, and unfortunately killed child. Despite volley got away apparently unharmed. Heading for London when last seen. Have closed Palace and cleared grounds."

It appears what actually happened was as follows:—

A Dr. David Pryce, a retired professor from one of the Scotch Universities, who lived in a house on Gipsy Hill, was taking a stroll down the central transept after dinner, when he was startled to hear the noise of breaking glass high up in the roof. Some large pieces of glass fell within a few yards of him into one of the ornamental fountains. Running to one side, he looked up, and saw that some heavy body had fallen on to the roof and coming through the glass was so balanced upon an iron girder. Even as he looked, the object broke away and fell with a frightening splash into the basin among the goldfish. Simultaneously he heard the crack of rifles firing in the grounds outside.

He was the first of the people round to run to the fountain, where he found, to his unspeakable horror, the bleeding body of a child, a sweet little girl of six, still almost breathing.

The news of this second victim was in the streets about ten

o'clock, and it was then that a real panic took possession of all the pleasure-seekers in Piccadilly and the Strand.

The special descriptive writers from the great daily papers, who went about the principal centres of amusement, witnessed the most extraordinary sights. Now and again there would be a false alarm that the dragon—for that is what people were beginning to call it—was in the neighbourhood, and there would be a stampede of men and women into the nearest place of shelter. The proprietor of one of the big Strand bars afterwards boasted that the panic had been worth an extra fifty pounds to him.

The Commissioner of Police became so seriously alarmed, both at the disorderly state of the streets, and the possible chance of another fatality, that he thought it wiser to obtain military assistance, and about half-past eleven London was practically under arms. Two or three linesmen were stationed at central points in the main streets, and little groups of cavalry with unslung carbines patrolled from place to place.

Although the strictest watch was kept all night, nothing was seen of the monster, but in the morning a constable of the C Division, detailed for special duty, found traces at the top of Ludgate Hill which proved conclusively that the animal had been there sometime during the night.

The Third Episode.

The wide-spread news that the terror had been in the very heart of London during the night created tremendous excitement among the authorities and the public at large. The City Police held a hurried consultation in Old Jewry about nine o'clock in the morning, and after hearing Sergeant Weatherley's account of his discovery, came to the conclusion that the dragon had probably made its lair on the top of St. Paul's Cathedral.

A man was at once sent round to the Deanery for a pass

which should allow a force of police to search the roofs, and came back in half an hour with an order written by Dean Gregory himself, requesting the officials to give the police every facility for a thorough examination.

It was then that the fatal mistake was made which added a fourth victim to the death roll.

About 9.30 a telegram was received at New Scotland Yard from a professional golfer at Mitcham, saying that some caddies on their way to the club-house had sighted the monster hovering over the Croydon road early in the morning. A wire was at once despatched to the local police station on the lower green, directing that strict inquiries should be made, and the result telegraphed at once. Meanwhile Scotland Yard communicated with Old Jewry, and the City Police made the incredible blunder of putting off the search party till the Mitcham report was thoroughly investigated.

It was not allowed to be known that the police had any suspicion that St. Paul's might harbour the dragon, and the fact of Sergeant Weatherley's discovery did not transpire till the second edition of the *Star* appeared, just about the time the final scene was being enacted on the south roof.

Accordingly the omnibuses followed the usual Cannon Street route, and the City men from the suburbs crowded them as usual. In the brilliant morning sunshine—for it was a perfect summer's day—it was extremely difficult to believe that anything untoward was afoot.

The panic of the night before, the panic of the gas lamps and the uncertain mystery of night, had very largely subsided. Many a city man who the night before had come out of the Alhambra or the Empire seized with a genuine terror, now sat on the top of his City 'bus smoking the after-breakfast cigarette and almost joking about the whole extraordinary affair. The fresh, new air was so delightful that it had its effect on everybody, and the police and soldiers who stood at ease round the statue of Queen Anne were saluted with a constant fire of chaff from the waggish young gentlemen of the Stock Exchange as they were carried to their daily work.

"What price the Dragon!" and "Have you got a muzzle handy!" resounded in the precincts of the Cathedral, and the merry witticisms afforded intense enjoyment to the crowds of ragamuffins who lounged round the top of Ludgate Hill.

Then, quite suddenly, came the last act of the terrible drama.

Just as a white Putney 'bus was slowly coming up the steep gradient of the hill, the horses straining and slipping on the road, a black object rose from behind the clock tower on the façade of the Cathedral, and with a long, easy dive the creature that was terrorising London came down upon the vehicle. It seemed to slide rapidly down the air with its wings poised and open, and it came straight at the omnibus. The driver, with great presence of mind and not a moment too soon, pulled his horses suddenly to the right, and the giant enemy rushed past with a great disturbance of the air hardly a yard away from the conveyance.

It sailed nearly down to the railway bridge before it was able to check its flight and turn.

Then, with a slow flapping of its great leathery wings, it came back to where the omnibus was oscillating violently as the horses reared and plunged.

It was the most horrible sight in the world. Seen at close quarters the monstrous creature was indescribably loathsome, and the stench from its body was overpowering. Its great horny beak was covered with brown stains, and in its eagerness and anger it was foaming and slobbering at the mouth. Its eyes, which were half-covered with a white scurf, had something of that malignant and horrible expression that one sometimes sees in the eyes of an evil-minded old man.

In a moment the thing was right over the omnibus, and the people on the top were hidden from view by the beating of its mighty wings. Three soldiers on the pavement in front of the Cathedral knelt down, and taking deliberate aim, fired almost simultaneously. A moment after the shots rang out, the horses, who had been squealing in an ecstasy of terror, overturned the vehicle. The dragon, which had been hit in the leather-like integument stretched between the rib-bones of its left wing, rose heavily and slowly, taking a little spring from the side of the omnibus, and giving utterance to a rapid choking sound, very like the gobbling of a turkey. Its wings beat the air with tremendous power, and with the regular sound of a pumping engine, and in its bill it held some bright red object, which was screaming in uncontrollable agony. In two seconds the creature had mounted above the horses, and all down Ludgate Hill the horror-bitten crowd could see that its writhing, screaming burden was a soldier of the line.

The man, by some curious instinct, had kept tight hold of his little swagger-stick, and his whirling arms bore a grotesque resemblance to the conductor of an orchestra directing its movements with his bâton. Some more shots pealed out, and the screaming stopped with the suddenness of a steam whistle turned off, while the swagger-stick fell down into the street.

Over the road, from house to house, was stretched a row of flags with a Union Jack in the centre, which had been put up earlier in the morning by an alderman who owned one of the shops, in order to signalise some important civic function. In mounting, the monster was caught by the line which supported the flags, and then with a tremendous effort it pulled the whole arrangement loose. Then, very slowly, and with the long row of gaudy flags streaming behind it, it rose high into the air and sank down behind the dome of St. Paul's. As it soared, regardless of the fusillade from below, it looked exactly like a fantastic Japanese kite. The whole affair, from the time of the first swoop from St. Paul's until the monster sank again to its refuge, only took two or three seconds over the minute.

The news of this fresh and terrible disaster reached the waiting party in Old Jewry almost immediately, and they started for the Cathedral without a moment's delay. They found Ludgate Hill was almost empty, as the police under the railway bridge were deflecting the traffic into other routes. On each side of the street hundreds of white faces peered from doorways and windows towards St. Paul's. The overturned omnibus still lay in the middle of the road, but the horses had been taken away.

The party marched in through the west door, and the ineffable peace of the great church fell round them like a cloak and made their business seem fantastic and unreal. Mr. Harding, the permanent clerk of the works, met them in the nave, and held a consultation with Lieutenant Boyle and Inspector Nicholson, who commanded the men. The clerk of the works produced a rough map of the various roofs, on any one of which the dragon might be. He suggested, and the lieutenant quite agreed, that two or three men should first be sent to try and locate the exact resting-place of the monster, and that afterwards the best shots should surround and attack it. The presence of a large number of men wandering about the extremely complicated system of approaches might well disturb the creature and send it abroad again. He himself, he added, would accompany the scouts.

Three men were chosen for the job, a sergeant of police and two soldiers. Mr. Harding took them into his office, and they removed their boots for greater convenience in climbing. They were conducted first of all into the low gallery hung with old frescoes which leads to the library, and then, opening a small door in the wall, Mr. Harding, beckoning the others to follow, disappeared into darkness.

They ascended some narrow winding steps deep into the thickness of the masonry, until a gleam of light showed stealing down from above, making their faces pale and haggard. Their leader stopped, and there was a jingling of keys. "It is unlikely it'll be here," he said in a low voice, "and anyway it can't get at us quickly, but be careful. Sergeant, you bring one man and come with me, and the last man stay behind and hold the door open in case we have to retreat." He turned the key in the lock and opened the narrow door.

For a moment the brilliant light of the sun blinded them, and then the two men who were yet a few steps down in the dark heard the other say, "Come on, it's all safe."

They came out into a large square court floored with lead. Great stone walls rose all around them, and the only outlet was the door by which they had come. It was exactly like a prison exercise yard, and towering away above their heads in front was the huge central dome. The dismal place was quite empty.

"The swine isn't here, that's certain," said one of the soldiers.

"No, we must go round to the south side," said the clerk of the works; "it's very much like this, only larger. But there's a better way to get to it. Let us go back at once."

They went down again to the library corridor, and turning by the archway debouching on the whispering gallery—they could hear the strains of the organ as they passed—went up another dark and narrow stairway. They came out onto a small ledge of stone, a kind of gutter, and there was very little room between the walls at their backs and the steep lead-covered side of the main roof which towered into the air straight in front.

"Now," said Mr. Harding, "we have got to climb up this slant and down the other side, and if he's anywhere about we shall see him there. At the bottom of the other slope is a gutter, like this, to stand in, but no wall, as it looks straight down into a big bear pit, like the one we went to first. We shall have to go right down the other slant, because if he's lying on the near side of the pit—and it's the shady side—we shan't be able to see him at all. You'll find it easy enough to get up, and if you should slip back this wall will bring you up short, but be very careful about going down. If you once begin to slide you'll toboggan right over the edge and on to the top of the beast, and even if he isn't there, it's a sixty foot drop."

As they climbed slowly up the steep roof, all London came into clear and lovely view—white, red, and purple in the sun. When at length they reached the top and clung there, for a moment, high in the air, like sparrows perching on the ridge of a house, they could only just see the mouth of the drop yawning down below them.

One of the soldiers, a lithe and athletic young fellow, was down at the bottom considerably before the others, and crouching in the broad gutter, he peered cautiously over the edge. They saw his shoulders heave with excitement, and in a moment he turned his head towards them. His face was white and his eyes full of loathing. They joined him at once, and the horror of what they saw will never leave any of the four.

The Dragon was lying on its side against the wall. Its whole vast length was heaving as if in pain, while close by it lay the remains of what was once a soldier of the Queen.

It was soon killed. The marksmen were hurriedly brought up from below, and after a perilous climb, owing to the weight of their rifles, lined the edge of the pit. They fired repeated volleys into the vast groaning creature. After the first volley it began to cough and choke, and vainly trying to open its maimed wings, dragged itself into the centre of the place. The mere sight of the malign thing gave a shock to the experience that was indescribable. It fulfilled no place in the order of life, and this fact induced a cold fear far more than its actual appearance. A psychologist who talked to one of the soldiers afterwards, got near to some fundamental truths dealing with the natural limits of sensation, in a brilliant article published in *Cosmopolis*. In its death agonies, agonies which were awful to look at, it crawled right across the floor of the court, and it moved the line of flags, which still remained fixed to one paw, in such a way that when they got down to it they found that, by a strange and pathetic coincidence, the Union Jack was covering the body of the dead soldier.

In this way the oldest living thing in the world was destroyed, and London breathed freely again.

Jack London

A Relic of the Pliocene

In 1897, during the chaotic Klondike Gold Rush, JACK LONDON
*(1876-1916) was amongst those who sought a fortune in the Yukon. The
character of life in the brutal landscapes of the north fueled much of his
subsequent fiction, including his most famous work,* The Call of the
Wild *(1903). A fascination with what was known as biological recapitulation—including the notion that the growing bodies of individuals
re-enact their evolutionary lineages, and that individuals can even tap
into the memories of ancestors—likewise haunted his work. In the words
of one scholar, London's writing tends "to expose the crack in modernity,
to show that it is not modern at all, or only insofar as it is also primitive,
a reprise."*[1] *"A Relic of the Pliocene" is the tall tale of mortal combat
between man and mammoth, between a relentless and old-fashioned
hunter and the lonely survivor of a prehistoric genus. It was published in
the prominent American magazine* Collier's Weekly *in January 1901,
and then collected in* The Faith of Men and Other Stories *(1904).*

I WASH my hands of him at the start. I cannot father his tales,
nor will I be responsible for them. I make these preliminary
reservations, observe, as a guard upon my own integrity. I possess a certain definite position in a small way, also a wife; and
for the good name of the community that honors my existence
with its approval, and for the sake of her posterity and mine, I

---

1 Michael Newton, "The Atavistic Nightmare: Memory and Recapitulation
in Jack London's Ghost and Fantasy Stories," in *The Oxford Handbook of Jack
London,* edited by Jay Williams (Oxford: Oxford University Press, 2017),
239-258 (240).

cannot take the chances I once did, nor foster probabilities with
the careless improvidence of youth. So, I repeat, I wash my
hands of him, this Nimrod, this mighty hunter, this homely,
blue-eyed, freckle-faced Thomas Stevens.

Having been honest to myself, and to whatever prospective
olive branches my wife may be pleased to tender me, I can now
afford to be generous. I shall not criticise the tales told me by
Thomas Stevens, and, further, I shall withhold my judgment.
If it be asked why, I can only add that judgment I have none.
Long have I pondered, weighed, and balanced, but never
have my conclusions been twice the same—forsooth! because
Thomas Stevens is a greater man than I. If he have told truths,
well and good; if untruths, still well and good. For who can
prove? or who disprove? I eliminate myself from the proposi-
tion, while those of little faith may do as I have done—go find
the same Thomas Stevens, and discuss to his face the various
matters which, if fortune serve, I shall relate. As to where he
may be found? The directions are simple: anywhere between 53
north latitude and the Pole, on the one hand; and, on the other,
the likeliest hunting grounds that lie between the east coast of
Siberia and farthermost Labrador. That he is there, somewhere,
within that clearly defined territory, I pledge the word of an
honorable man whose expectations entail straight speaking and
right living.

Thomas Stevens may have toyed prodigiously with truth,
but when we first met (it were well to mark this point), he
wandered into my camp when I thought myself a thousand
miles beyond the outermost post of civilization. At the sight
of his human face, the first in weary months, I could have
sprung forward and folded him in my arms (and I am not by
any means a demonstrative man); but to him his visit seemed
the most casual thing under the sun. He just strolled into the
light of my camp, passed the time of day after the custom of
men on beaten trails, threw my snowshoes the one way and a

couple of dogs the other, and so made room for himself by the fire. Said he'd just dropped in to borrow a pinch of soda and to see if I had any decent tobacco. He plucked forth an ancient pipe, loaded it with painstaking care, and, without as much as by your leave, whacked half the tobacco of my pouch into his. Yes, the stuff was fairly good. He sighed with the contentment of the just, and literally absorbed the smoke from the crisping yellow flakes, and it did my smoker's heart good to behold him.

Hunter? Trapper? Prospector? He shrugged his shoulders. No; just sort of knocking round a bit. Had come up from the Great Slave some time since, and was thinking of trapsing over into the Yukon country. The Factor of Koshim had spoken about the discoveries on the Klondike, and he was of a mind to run over for a peep. I noticed that he spoke of the Klondike in the archaic vernacular, calling it the Reindeer River—a conceited custom that the Old Timers employ against the *che-cha-quas* and all tenderfeet in general. But he did it so naïvely and as such a matter of course, that there was no sting, and I forgave him. He also had it in view, he said, before he crossed the divide into the Yukon, to make a little run up Fort o' Good Hope way.

Now Fort o' Good Hope is a far journey to the north, over and beyond the Circle, in a place where the feet of few men have trod; and when a nondescript ragamuffin comes in out of the night, from nowhere in particular, to sit by one's fire and discourse on such in terms of "trapsing" and "a little run," it is fair time to rouse up and shake off the dream. Wherefore I looked about me; saw the fly, and, underneath, the pine boughs spread for the sleeping furs; saw the grub sacks, the camera, the frosty breaths of the dogs circling on the edge of the light; and, above, a great streamer of the aurora bridging the zenith from southeast to northwest. I shivered. There is a magic in the Northland night, that steals in on one like fevers from malarial marshes. You are clutched and downed before you are aware. Then I looked to the snowshoes, lying prone and crossed where he had flung them. Also I had an eye to my tobacco pouch. Half, at least, of its goodly store had vamosed. That settled it. Fancy had not tricked me after all.

Crazed with suffering, I thought, looking steadfastly at the man—one of those wild stampeders, strayed far from his bearings and wandering like a lost soul through great vastnesses and unknown deeps. Oh, well, let his moods slip on, until, mayhap, he gathers his tangled wits together. Who knows?—the mere sound of a fellow-creature's voice may bring all straight again.

So I led him on in talk, and soon I marvelled, for he talked of game and the ways thereof. He had killed the Siberian wolf of westernmost Alaska, and the chamois in the secret Rockies. He averred he knew the haunts where the last buffalo still roamed; that he had hung on the flanks of the caribou when they ran by the hundred thousand, and slept in the Great Barrens on the musk-ox's winter trail.

And I shifted my judgment accordingly (the first revision, but by no account the last), and deemed him a monumental effigy of truth. Why it was I know not, but the spirit moved me to repeat a tale told to me by a man who had dwelt in the land too long to know better. It was of the great bear that hugs the steep slopes of St. Elias, never descending to the levels of the gentler inclines. Now God so constituted this creature for its hillside habitat that the legs of one side are all of a foot longer than those of the other. This is mighty convenient, as will be readily admitted. So I hunted this rare beast in my own name, told it in the first person, present tense, painted the requisite locale, gave it the necessary garnishings and touches of verisimilitude, and looked to see the man stunned by the recital.

Not he. Had he doubted, I could have forgiven him. Had he objected, denying the dangers of such a hunt by virtue of the animal's inability to turn about and go the other way—had he done this, I say, I could have taken him by the hand for the true sportsman that he was. Not he. He sniffed, looked on me, and sniffed again; then gave my tobacco due praise, thrust one foot into my lap, and bade me examine the gear. It was a *mucluc* of the Innuit pattern, sewed together with sinew threads, and devoid of beads or furbelows. But it was the skin itself that was remarkable. In that it was all of half an inch thick, it reminded me of walrus-hide; but there the resemblance ceased, for no walrus ever bore so marvellous a growth of hair. On the side and ankles this hair was well-nigh worn away, what of friction with underbrush and snow; but around the top and down the more sheltered back it was coarse, dirty black, and very thick. I parted it with difficulty and looked beneath for the fine fur that is common with northern animals, but found it in this case to be absent. This, however, was compensated for by the length. Indeed, the tufts that had survived wear and tear measured all of seven or eight inches.

I looked up into the man's face, and he pulled his foot down and asked, "Find hide like that on your St. Elias bear?"

I shook my head. "Nor on any other creature of land or sea," I answered candidly. The thickness of it, and the length of the hair, puzzled me.

"That," he said, and said without the slightest hint of impressiveness, "that came from a mammoth."

"Nonsense!" I exclaimed, for I could not forbear the protest of my unbelief. "The mammoth, my dear sir, long ago vanished from the earth. We know it once existed by the fossil remains that we have unearthed, and by a frozen carcass that the Siberian sun saw fit to melt from out the bosom of a glacier; but we also know that no living specimen exists. Our explorers—"

At this word he broke in impatiently. "Your explorers? Pish! A weakly breed. Let us hear no more of them. But tell me, O man, what you may know of the mammoth and his ways."

Beyond contradiction, this was leading to a yarn; so I baited my hook by ransacking my memory for whatever data I possessed on the subject in hand. To begin with, I emphasized that the animal was prehistoric, and marshalled all my facts in support of this. I mentioned the Siberian sand bars that abounded with ancient mammoth bones; spoke of the large quantities of fossil ivory purchased from the Innuits by the Alaska Commercial Company; and acknowledged having myself mined six- and eight-foot tusks from the pay gravel of the Klondike creeks. "All fossils," I concluded, "found in the midst of débris deposited through countless ages."

"I remember when I was a kid," Thomas Stevens sniffed (he had a most confounded way of sniffing), "that I saw a petrified watermelon. Hence, though mistaken persons sometimes delude themselves into thinking that they are really raising or eating them, there are no such things as extant watermelons."

"But the question of food," I objected, ignoring his point, which was puerile and without bearing. "The soil must bring forth vegetable life in lavish abundance to support such monstrous creations. Nowhere in the North is the soil so prolific. Ergo, the mammoth cannot exist."

"I pardon your ignorance concerning many matters of this Northland, for you are a young man and have travelled little; but, at the same time, I am inclined to agree with you on one thing. The mammoth no longer exists. How do I know? I killed the last one with my own right arm."

Thus spake Nimrod, the Mighty Hunter. I threw a stick of firewood at the dogs and bade them quit their unholy howling, and waited. Undoubtedly this liar of singular felicity would open his mouth and requite me for my St. Elias bear.

"It was this way," he at last began, after the appropriate silence had intervened. "I was in camp one day—"

"Where?" I interrupted.

He waved his hand vaguely in the direction of the northeast, where stretched a terra incognita into which vastness few men have strayed and fewer emerged. "I was in camp one day with Klooch. Klooch was as handsome a little *kamooks* as ever whined betwixt the traces or shoved nose into a camp kettle. Her father was a full-blood Malemute from Russian Pastilik on Bering Sea, and I bred her, and with understanding, out of a clean-legged bitch of the Hudson Bay stock. I tell you, O man, she was a corker combination. And now, on this day I have in mind, she was brought to pup through a pure wild wolf of the woods—gray, and long of limb, with big lungs and no end of staying powers. Say! Was there ever the like? It was a new breed of dog I had started, and I could look forward to big things.

"As I have said, she was brought neatly to pup, and safely delivered. I was squatting on my hams over the litter—seven sturdy, blind little beggars—when from behind came a bray of trumpets and crash of brass. There was a rush, like the wind-squall that kicks the heels of the rain, and I was midway to my feet when knocked flat on my face. At the same instant I heard Klooch sigh, very much as a man does when you've planted your fist in his belly. You can stake your sack I lay quiet, but I twisted my head around and saw a huge bulk swaying above me. Then the blue sky flashed into view and I got to my feet. A hairy mountain of flesh was just disappearing in the underbrush on the edge of the open. I caught a rear-end glimpse, with a stiff tail, as big in girth as my body, standing out straight behind. The next second only a tremendous hole remained in the thicket, though I could still hear the sounds as of a tornado dying quickly away, underbrush ripping and tearing, and trees snapping and crashing.

"I cast about for my rifle. It had been lying on the ground with the muzzle against a log; but now the stock was smashed, the barrel out of line, and the working-gear in a thousand bits. Then I looked for the slut, and—and what do you suppose?"

I shook my head.

"May my soul burn in a thousand hells if there was anything left of her! Klooch, the seven sturdy, blind little beggars— gone, all gone. Where she had stretched was a slimy, bloody depression in the soft earth, all of a yard in diameter, and around the edges a few scattered hairs."

I measured three feet on the snow, threw about it a circle, and glanced at Nimrod.

"The beast was thirty long and twenty high," he answered, "and its tusks scaled over six times three feet. I couldn't believe, myself, at the time, for all that it had just happened. But if my senses had played me, there was the broken gun and the hole in the brush. And there was—or, rather, there was not—Klooch and the pups. O man, it makes me hot all over now when I think of it. Klooch! Another Eve! The mother of a new race! And a rampaging, ranting, old bull mammoth, like a second flood, wiping them, root and branch, off the face of the earth! Do you wonder that the blood-soaked earth cried out to high God? Or that I grabbed the hand-axe and took the trail?"

"The hand-axe?" I exclaimed, startled out of myself by the picture. "The hand-axe, and a big bull mammoth, thirty feet long, twenty feet—"

Nimrod joined me in my merriment, chuckling gleefully. "Wouldn't it kill you?" he cried. "Wasn't it a beaver's dream? Many's the time I've laughed about it since, but at the time it was no laughing matter, I was that danged mad, what of the gun and Klooch. Think of it, O man! A brand-new, unclassified, uncopyrighted breed, and wiped out before ever it opened its eyes or took out its intention papers! Well, so be it. Life's full of disappointments, and rightly so. Meat is best after a famine, and a bed soft after a hard trail.

"As I was saying, I took out after the beast with the hand-axe, and hung to its heels down the valley; but when he circled back toward the head, I was left winded at the lower end. Speaking of grub, I might as well stop long enough to explain a couple of points. Up thereabouts, in the midst of the mountains, is an almighty curious formation. There is no end of little valleys, each like the other much as peas in a pod, and all neatly tucked away with straight, rocky walls rising on all sides. And at the lower ends are always small openings where the drainage or glaciers must have broken out. The only way in is through these mouths, and they are all small, and some smaller than others. As to grub—you've slushed around on the rain-soaked islands of the Alaskan coast down Sitka way, most likely, seeing as you're a traveller. And you know how stuff grows there— big, and juicy, and jungly. Well, that's the way it was with those valleys. Thick, rich soil, with ferns and grasses and such things in patches higher than your head. Rain three days out of four during the summer months; and food in them for a thousand mammoths, to say nothing of small game for man.

"But to get back. Down at the lower end of the valley I got winded and gave over. I began to speculate, for when my wind left me my dander got hotter and hotter, and I knew I'd never know peace of mind till I dined on roasted mammoth-foot. And I knew, also, that that stood for *skookum mamook pukapuk*— excuse Chinook, I mean there was a big fight coming. Now the mouth of my valley was very narrow, and the walls steep. High up on one side was one of those big pivot rocks, or balancing rocks, as some call them, weighing all of a couple of hundred tons. Just the thing. I hit back for camp, keeping an eye open so the bull couldn't slip past, and got my ammunition. It wasn't worth anything with the rifle smashed; so I opened the shells, planted the powder under the rock, and touched it off with slow fuse. Wasn't much of a charge, but the old boulder tilted up lazily and dropped down into place, with just space enough to let the creek drain nicely. Now I had him."

"But how did you have him?" I queried. "Who ever heard of a man killing a mammoth with a hand-axe? And, for that matter, with anything else?"

"O man, have I not told you I was mad?" Nimrod replied, with a slight manifestation of sensitiveness. "Mad clean through, what of Klooch and the gun? Also, was I not a hunter?

And was this not new and most unusual game? A hand-axe? Pish! I did not need it. Listen, and you shall hear of a hunt, such as might have happened in the youth of the world when caveman rounded up the kill with hand-axe of stone. Such would have served me as well. Now is it not a fact that man can outwalk the dog or horse? That he can wear them out with the intelligence of his endurance?"

I nodded.

"Well?"

The light broke in on me, and I bade him continue.

"My valley was perhaps five miles around. The mouth was closed. There was no way to get out. A timid beast was that bull mammoth, and I had him at my mercy. I got on his heels again, hollered like a fiend, pelted him with cobbles, and raced him around the valley three times before I knocked off for supper. Don't you see? A race-course! A man and a mammoth! A hippodrome, with sun, moon, and stars to referee!

"It took me two months to do it, but I did it. And that's no beaver dream. Round and round I ran him, me travelling on the inner circle, eating jerked meat and salmon berries on the run, and snatching winks of sleep between. Of course, he'd get desperate at times and turn. Then I'd head for soft ground where the creek spread out, and lay anathema upon him and his ancestry, and dare him to come on. But he was too wise to bog in a mud puddle. Once he pinned me in against the walls, and I crawled back into a deep crevice and waited. Whenever he felt for me with his trunk, I'd belt him with the hand-axe till he pulled out, shrieking fit to split my ear drums, he was that mad. He knew he had me and didn't have me, and it near drove him wild. But he was no man's fool. He knew he was safe as long as I stayed in the crevice, and he made up his mind to keep me there. And he was dead right, only he hadn't figured on the commissary. There was neither grub nor water around that spot, so on the face of it he couldn't keep up the siege. He'd stand before the opening for hours, keeping an eye on me and flapping mosquitoes away with his big blanket ears. Then the thirst would come on him and he'd ramp round and roar till the earth shook, calling me every name he could lay tongue to. This was to frighten me, of course; and when he thought I was sufficiently impressed, he'd back away softly and try to make a sneak for the creek. Sometimes I'd let him get almost there—only a couple of hundred yards away it was—when out I'd pop and back he'd come, lumbering along like the old landslide he was. After I'd done this a few times, and he'd figured it out, he changed his tactics. Grasped the time element, you see. Without a word of warning, away he'd go, tearing for the water like mad, scheming to get there and back before I ran away. Finally, after cursing me most horribly, he raised the siege and deliberately stalked off to the water-hole.

"That was the only time he penned me,—three days of it,—but after that the hippodrome never stopped. Round, and round, and round, like a six days' go-as-I-please, for he never pleased. My clothes went to rags and tatters, but I never stopped to mend, till at last I ran naked as a son of earth, with nothing but the old hand-axe in one hand and a cobble in the other. In fact, I never stopped, save for peeps of sleep in the crannies and ledges of the cliffs. As for the bull, he got perceptibly thinner and thinner—must have lost several tons at least—and as nervous as a schoolmarm on the wrong side of matrimony. When I'd come up with him and yell, or lam him with a rock at long range, he'd jump like a skittish colt and tremble all over. Then he'd pull out on the run, tail and trunk waving stiff, head over one shoulder and wicked eyes blazing, and the way he'd swear at me was something dreadful. A most immoral beast he was, a murderer, and a blasphemer.

"But towards the end he quit all this, and fell to whimpering and crying like a baby. His spirit broke and he became a quivering jelly-mountain of misery. He'd get attacks of palpitation

of the heart, and stagger around like a drunken man, and fall
down and bark his shins. And then he'd cry, but always on the
run. O man, the gods themselves would have wept with him,
and you yourself or any other man. It was pitiful, and there
was so much of it, but I only hardened my heart and hit up the
pace. At last I wore him clean out, and he lay down, broken-
winded, broken-hearted, hungry, and thirsty. When I found
he wouldn't budge, I hamstrung him, and spent the better part
of the day wading into him with the hand-axe, he a-sniffing
and sobbing till I worked in far enough to shut him off. Thirty
feet long he was, and twenty high, and a man could sling a ham-
mock between his tusks and sleep comfortably. Barring the fact
that I had run most of the juices out of him, he was fair eating,
and his four feet, alone, roasted whole, would have lasted a man
a twelvemonth. I spent the winter there myself."

"And where is this valley?" I asked

He waved his hand in the direction of the northeast, and
said: "Your tobacco is very good. I carry a fair share of it in
my pouch, but I shall carry the recollection of it until I die.
In token of my appreciation, and in return for the moccasins
on your own feet, I will present to you these *muclucs*. They
commemorate Klooch and the seven blind little beggars. They
are also souvenirs of an unparalleled event in history, namely,
the destruction of the oldest breed of animal on earth, and the
youngest. And their chief virtue lies in that they will never
wear out."

Having effected the exchange, he knocked the ashes from his
pipe, gripped my hand good night, and wandered off through
the snow. Concerning this tale, for which I have already dis-
claimed responsibility, I would recommend those of little faith
to make a visit to the Smithsonian Institute. If they bring the
requisite credentials and do not come in vacation time, they
will undoubtedly gain an audience with Professor Dolvid-
son. The *muclucs* are in his possession, and he will verify, not

the manner in which they were obtained, but the material of which they are composed. When he states that they are made from the skin of the mammoth, the scientific world accepts his verdict. What more would you have?

James Barr

The Man in Moccasins

Unlike most other items in this collection, this murky story, printed in the Strand Magazine *in August 1905, draws attention to the status of fossils as contested natural resources. Their excavation was by no means unconnected to the ruthless extraction of more obviously utilitarian sources of mineral wealth. The author,* JAMES BARR (1862-1923), *was a Canadian journalist and novelist who also wrote under the name Angus Evan Abbott. The literary output of Barr, who spent much of his career in London, indicates the characteristic diversity of the turn-of-the-century popular magazines, and includes many tales of the Canadian wilderness, the adventures of highwaymen, and compilations of American humor.*

THE man in moccasins was shown in.

"I call to ask you to believe a story that is beyond your power to believe," he said, quietly.

Sir Silas Martin, lumber king and British knight, nodded.

"I am an Englishman. I tell you this to convince you that I lack the imagination needed for the concoction of an utter untruth."

Again Sir Silas nodded a non-committal nod to the man in moccasins. At the same time his lips curled sceptically. The man in moccasins noticed the curl.

"Let me put it in this way—I understand the proportion of things. I, an Englishman, would not attempt to bamboozle you, an American."

Sir Silas's brow darkened a little at this allusion to the land of his birth. He was an American, one who had quitted his native state to take up lumbering in Canada. Fortune had approved of him, forests fell prostrate to fill his pockets, and finally, to gild his career, came a knighthood. He accepted this distinction as he accepted everything of pride or profit that came his way, and went on with his money-getting and his giving in charity.

For the third time he contented himself with a nod.

"I say I lack the conceit to attempt to bamboozle you," asserted the man in moccasins, a hint of impatience in his tones not lost upon the millionaire.

"It has been done," acknowledged Sir Silas.

"I, for one, will not try. To be frank with you, I desire to tell you a story that is beyond your belief. Nevertheless it is true. I trust to its very impossibility to assist me in winning your attention. May I begin?"

"Sit down," said Sir Silas.

The man in moccasins dropped a huge slouch hat on the floor and whirled a chair to a suitable position. Outside the July sun smote down upon Montreal, each ray a fierce-flung javelin tipped with fire. After the clangour and swelter of the streets Sir Silas Martin's office seemed a cool and quiet haven. The stranger was lean for an Englishman. He wore a blue woollen shirt, patched and frayed; knee-breeches, they, too, decidedly the worse for wear; thick French-Canadian stockings, and rough-hewn moccasins. His hair was long, his face and hands tanned to the colour of an old oak chest. He straddled his legs and, locking his hands together, jammed his forearms like a wedge between his knees, dropping his shoulders as one who sits on a stile. Sir Silas shoved his chair from the desk and throwing his shoulders back tilted the seat as far as the springs would allow it to go. For some moments the two men looked at each other, eye to eye. The man in moccasins spoke.

"Sir Silas, I have been into the heart of the wilderness."

He jerked his head towards the north.

"I have been in the wilderness and I have come out. You know the fringe of those awful wilds which stretch from the St. Lawrence and Ottawa away to Hudson Bay and beyond. The fringe has been good to you, it is told."

He paused, and, after a time, Sir Silas nodded his inscrutable nod.

"So I have been told. But, Sir Silas, it has in reserve for you still greater things. It has given you, chip by chip, fortune and, bit by bit, fame of a sort. Of a *sort*, I repeat. It holds for you fame of quite another sort. I have been into the heart of the wilderness and I know."

"You are not giving yourself all this trouble solely for my good, I take it?"

"By no means," replied the man in moccasins.

"I am glad there is something of self in the matter."

The man in moccasins thought a moment.

"No; I acknowledge nothing of the kind. There is nothing of self in the trouble I am taking, as you will find at the end. I will profit in no way; no, not in any way. Others will."

"Others in whom you have an interest, I take it?"

"You take too much. I have interest in no one on earth, not even in myself."

The millionaire threw up his head impatiently.

"I trust there is no part of your story harder to believe than this you have just now told me," he said. His tones were sarcastic.

"There is, I assure you. If you have finished cross-examining I will go on with my evidence-in-chief."

The millionaire fell back upon his non-committal nod.

"In May of this year a comrade and I launched a canoe on Lac des Quinze, a sheet of water you may remember, for many millions of feet of your best lumber came from its shores. From the Quinze we proceed to Lake Abitibi, and from that shallow lake we pushed on into the unsurveyed wilds, holding to an easterly course. We got a certain distance. If I find at the end of your account that you are sufficiently interested, I will tell you definitely where we got to. At present I content myself with saying that we won a certain distance. It was hard work. It was slow work. We ran against a great many portages across which we were obliged to cut out a rough way, for no Indian trapper's moccasin pads the bank of the river along which we made our way. Moreover, we were prospecting as we went along, and prospecting takes time."

"If you are about to attempt to interest me in a mine, let me tell you that you are wasting your time."

"Pray allow me to believe that I know what I am about. I would not dream of mentioning 'mine' to you. You are a lumberman."

"My remark applies equally to lumber."

"I know nothing of lumber and desire to continue to know nothing of lumber. May I go on?"

Sir Silas Martin nodded.

"We had weary work of it, day after day, seeing nothing but those interminable wilds and each the face of the other. I fear we grew to hate each other's presence with an intense hatred."

"Where is your companion now?"

"He is up in the region awaiting my return."

"You intend to return?"

"It is to accomplish the return journey that I am here submitting, with more impatience than is warranted, I fancy, to your cross-examination."

"Why did you leave him?"

"To tell you my tale."

"Go on."

"The savagery, the dismay, the oppression, the forebodings of the wilderness wore into our souls, so that neither of us spoke for days at a time. You see, Sir Silas, it was our first break away from civilization. But it so befell that one afternoon we happened upon a rather remarkable place. A huge amphitheatre it was, worn out of the rock by a great fall that roared over against our entrance. The banks of this place were high and covered with timber, save in one place where the rock sloped bare for twenty yards down to the water. Our canoe was caught by a backwater, and we floated up to the cheek of the fall, where we stepped ashore.

"I saw at a glance that my companion had made up his mind to camp there for the night, although there were still many hours of daylight before us. He soon had a smudge smoking, for the black fly was desperate. You know how desperate the black fly can be! I followed his lead, lighting my smudge at a distance from his, and there we sat, each as morose and savage as a Malay about to run amuck. You know the Quebec wildernesses with their black fly and their dull, drawing pain of mute despair?"

The millionaire nodded.

"Yes, yes. Only those who have penetrated the land know what that chaos of water and rock and spruce really is. Now it came to pass that after a time, as if by a common impulse, the two of us arose and set out to stroll round our side of the amphitheatre, each heading for where the rock sloped gently down to the water. My companion took the high part of the bank; I walked by the marge of the stream. Suddenly we each put our foot on the thing, I claim, simultaneously. One glance sufficed, and we stood looking at one another.

" 'My find,' savagely barked my companion down at me. 'It's mine.'

" 'Mine,' I bellowed back.

"Instantly we drew revolvers and simultaneously we shot."

The man in moccasins paused to laugh a hearty roar of laughter. Sir Silas smiled in sympathy.

"The lonesomeness had made us mad, but the explosion

of our pistols cleared the air like a thunderstorm. Before the echoes ceased their crazy shuttling to and fro across that amphitheatre I had my companion by the hand and we were at once such friends as never were. I had a very narrow shave, as you can see."

He threw open the breast of his woollen shirt and revealed an unhealed sore along his side on a level with his heart.

"A narrow escape," admitted the millionaire, warming up a little. "I hope you and your companion are not given to disputing often."

"It was a wholesome lesson to each of us," acknowledged the man in moccasins.

"What was it you each claimed?"

"I will tell you. Down the bank where, as I have said, the rock slopes gently to the stream there lay a wonderful thing, its tail reaching far into the water. The body of it ran up the bank and disappeared into the woods. One glance satisfied me that I had come upon a monster reptile of prehistoric ages, let into the dull rock of the bank."

Sir Silas Martin placed his hands to his sides, threw back his head, and roared in laughter.

"You are a magazine story in being," gasped the knight. "I read you from four to six times a year, and gaze upon you in illustrations as you stand horror-bound, fear-stricken, before some wonderful prehistoric creature of monster dimensions. You have stepped out of the pages of some magazine. I have paid ten cents for you. I say I bought you for ten cents off some news stand."

"Be it so. All I ask of you is that you read me to the very end," said the man in moccasins.

"Was your reptile alive?"

"No. Fossil."

Again Sir Silas went off into a spasm of laughter.

"You are spoiling what might be a good story," he cried.

"When you were about it you should have made the reptile alive."

"Why should I?" demanded the Englishman, quietly.

"Well, you see, you were quite as likely to find the thing alive as in fossil in Laurentian rock. Laurentian rock belongs to life's earliest dawn, that dim period of the invertebrate. Your reptile has a backbone?"

"It is all backbone."

"In Laurentian rock cannot be found anything with backbone," said Sir Silas, definitely.

"Once upon a time the world was flat."

"That was before the days of Ananias. Since his day it has been far from flat for those who choose to listen."

The fingers of the man in moccasins raked along the carpet till they came in contact with the rim of his hat.

"I fancy I have made a mistake in coming to you," he began, at the same time making as if to arise. Sir Silas hastened to say:—

"Sit still. Don't think of going. I am just getting interested, and would like to hear you out."

"I am not here to amuse you."

"My dear sir, you are more than amusing; you are utterly impossible. But go ahead. If you can convince me of a fossil reptile in Laurentian rock I want to hear you out."

"I am not trying to convince you. In the beginning I told you that my story is beyond the power of your mind to believe."

"Overlook the shortcomings of my power of mind for a minute. You tell me that there is a reptile plainly discernible in the rock?"

"It may be the fossil of a long-necked sea-lizard or plesio-saurus. I am not saying that it is."

Sir Silas raised his brows.

"You know something of extinct reptiles, then?"

"I received what is called an 'education' at Cambridge."

"Did that education reach so deep down as to convince you

that remains of high forms of life cannot be found in the oldest type of rock?"

"It did; but since stepping out into the world I have been obliged to throw over more than one conviction convinced into me, if I may use the expression, at Cambridge."

The millionaire swung half circles in his chair for a few moments before asking:—

"How did you chance to come to me with this—this—well, as you are rather tetchy, call it 'information'?"

"I ascertained the records of wealthy Montrealers and found that you were not only a millionaire, but also a member of the Palæontological Society of Great Britain. I sought the combination of specific knowledge of fossils and ample resources in gold. I thought I found this fusion in you."

"What do you require of my knowledge of fossils?"

"I require it only to interest you in my find. If it does that it may help me to a little of your wealth."

"That's frank, at least. What amount of my wealth do you want to be helped to, and for what purpose?"

The man in moccasins rose to his feet. He gave no direct answer to the question.

"Sir Silas, I have no means of knowing whether you are really a learned man or not. I judge that you are not. I take it that you are a member of the Palæontological Society for the same reason that you are a knight—vanity. Undoubtedly you are a skilled lumberman. I see that you began at the bottom of the tree and are now seated on the apex of the world's lumber pile, and it occurs to me that in the scramble to your present position you had not the leisure to go deep into the subject of fossils. You would like to be learned, I have no doubt; but that being out of the question you would now like to be considered as learned in the subject."

Sir Silas gazed upon the man in moccasins from under his eyebrows. He wondered if this strange Englishman guessed

that palæontology was the one enthralling study of his, and
hoped, by casting a slur on his knowledge of that ology, to spur
him to follow after the thing said to be in the wilderness.

"You have been a great success," continued the man in moccasins. "You have laid the foundations well and truly, you have
built the walls, flung the fan vaultings and the flying buttresses
fearlessly, and, in a manner, roofed a most imposing edifice—
your career. You have now the chance to rear the commanding
dome upon whose giant proportions the sun of fame may blaze
so that he blinks the eye of the world."

"Chaos crash upon your gilded dome," exclaimed the millionaire, violently. He leaped to his feet and began to pace the
room excitedly. "What is it you want of me? Don't shove fame
into my face nor prattle of blinding suns and blinking worlds.
Are you telling me the truth when you tell me of a reptile in the
rock? What in thunder do you want of me?"

"I want you to come with me to see the reptile in the rock."

"You want more!"

"Yes; I want money."

"How much?"

"One thousand dollars will be ample."

" 'Will be ample'! That expression implies that the money is
not wanted as payment for a service rendered, but is needed for
a specific purpose?"

"You are an observant man, Sir Silas."

"What is the purpose?"

"That you will learn at the end. The purpose, I may say, is all
to your advantage."

"I am not accustomed to having things so wholly to my
advantage as you seem to have arranged. So many advantages
lead my mind to a state of wonderment. I suppose you can see
some rebuffs awaiting me if I agree to your proposal?"

"Sir, I must continue to speak the truth. I fail to see where
you can meet with any rebuff, however small."

"Your friend? He is as much entitled to payment for the find as you?"

"The money I ask of you is all for him. I told you some time ago that I have no interest in the matter, and sought for no advantage from the find."

Sir Silas Martin paused, shoved his hands deep into his pockets, and frowned at his open desk for a minute or more. Then he switched his eyes on to the face of the man in moccasins. "I'll go," he suddenly exclaimed, and sitting down he drew forth his cheque-book. "What name?" he asked.

"Please draw the cheque in favour of yourself and send a clerk to cash it," said the man in moccasins.

"I will be ready to accompany you this day week. Where shall I meet you?"

"At Mattawa, on the Canadian Pacific Railway," replied the man in moccasins.

The millionaire took the wad of bills from his clerk and held them towards the Englishman. He said: "I part with this money saying, 'Silas Martin, you—confounded fool.'"

The man in moccasins slipped the wad into his pocket, clapped on his hat, and, saying nothing more than "Good-day," passed out into the street. At the corner of the street the man in moccasins came upon a small boy, who raised a thin, piping voice in an endeavour to sell newspapers. Into the little chap's hand he slipped a five-dollar bill and passed on. Next he dived into a ready-made clothes store, from which he came forth dressed like an ordinary citizen. That same evening he took passage on a little steamer, and early next morning found himself in Quebec, city of perpendiculars. He scrambled about her slopes and slants until the hour of opening offices came, when he presented himself before one of the best-known lawyers.

"I want you to register for me certain claims—mining, power, and timber. Those three claims will cover everything I find in and on the ground taken up, I suppose? Very well. As the district in which I desire rights is as yet unsurveyed I have myself drawn maps of it."

He unrolled two maps, one of them supplemented by half-a-dozen sketches. Maps and sketches were as if drawn by an artist.

"This," he said to the solicitor, "is a map of the route from Abitibi to the plot of land over which I desire rights. Roughly, two hundred miles, I make it. This," picking up the second sheet of tracing paper, "is a map of the particular spot I wish to possess. There can be no mistaking the place, for in these," lifting the six sketches, "I give pictures of various objects that are not likely to change. Here is a particularly splendid birch tree, is it not? Look at it! I have never seen a more glorious specimen. There is no such lovable tree as the birch, the shepherd of the wilds. Here are the falls; this the amphitheatre of water, with its sullen backwaters and centre of raging rapids shown; this a peculiarly-marked face of rock. No one can mistake the place having these before him."

The lawyer acknowledged this.

"Now, here is the section of which I desire the mining rights. I am merely a professional prospector and must register the property in the names of my employers. Here are the names, and I suppose you can work the matter?"

He passed over a paper on which was written: "Ann Grace Fullerton, widow, Midhurst, in the County of Sussex, England; the Palæontological Society of Great Britain, headquarters, London, England; Sir Silas Martin, Knight, lumberman and capitalist, Montreal, Province of Quebec, Canada. Equal shares."

Three days later the Englishman, once again in moccasins, put up at Rosemont House in Mattawa, made all arrangements for the coming journey, and spent every moment of his leisure time in practising with a bow he had bought from an Indian.

The midday mid-August sun beat down upon the chaos of

woods and waters and rocks in far Northern Quebec, his rays, in their fierceness, scintillating like diamonds in the air. Along the gorge through which one river flowed rumbled the sullen sound of the falling of great waters. Ethereal fantasies in foam floated on the bosom of the stream, proud and white as swans, and bubbles flashed their fairy flames as they danced along, for truly the children of the falls leave the place of their birth resplendently apparelled. Skirting the bank, feeling for still waters, rode two canoes, each paddled by two Indians. In the waist of the first canoe sat the man in moccasins. The second canoe bore Sir Silas Martin, looking the lumberman he was, if not the millionaire. Since leaving Abitibi, now eight days ago, the spirits of the man in moccasins had been exuberant. He laughed, he sang, he told tales, and made himself genial to millionaire and Indian alike. Ashore he would practise with that bow of his, and had become so skilled in its use that he could knock over the silly Canadian "partridge" with great certainty, and on rarer occasions managed to bag a rabbit which the mute mongrel he had bought off an Indian at Abitibi nosed out of its retreat. But on this, the last day of the journey, a sudden change came over him. He grew silent to the verge of the morose. Not a word had he spoken to man or beast all the morning. When the rumble of the falls grew large he found tongue.

"We are at our journey's end, Sir Silas," he said.

"It has been a long journey, but I have enjoyed it," replied the millionaire. "I find that the wilderness is still a large part of me."

"Keep to the right," said the man in moccasins, addressing the paddlers.

Presently the canoes shot out into a great circle of water ringed round with rocks and trees. Down the centre rushed a torrent, flinging and fuming at the tousling of the falls that unceasingly drummed their reverberating, hollow, deep-tongued drum. Spray fine as witch-mist blew from the turmoil to drift away and lose itself in the green of the woods. To the sweep of a backwater the canoes skirted the bank.

Suddenly the man in moccasins pointed to the shore.

"There is your petrified reptile, sir."

The millionaire, whose gaze had been sweeping the encircling bank, glanced eagerly in the direction indicated by the man in moccasins. There, as though let into the sombre rock by a Titan worker in mosaics, lay a mighty seam of sand-white material, this streaked and mottled, ribbed and ringed, by patches of dull yellow. From beneath the lap of the ripples he could follow the thing as it rose, heaving up the long slope of the bank until, diving, it disappeared under the roots of the spruce and balsam. Sir Silas Martin said no word, but kept his eyes on the whiteness until he stepped ashore at the foot of the falls. Then, hands in pockets, he strolled over until his feet rested on the glistening surface. He toed a seam of the yellow. The man in moccasins stood beside him.

"Quartz?" asked the millionaire.

"Quartz," answered the man in moccasins.

"Gold?"

"Gold."

"You have had it assayed?"

"Yes."

Sir Silas slowly scrambled up the slope, following a rude-run trail, and at a distance of fifty yards came upon a hole sunk some four feet into ground, exposing a square yard of quartz as rich as that on the shore. He returned to the marge of the stream and confronted the man in moccasins.

"Is this the reptile?"

"It is."

"You will take no exception to my mentioning the name of Ananias now?"

"I will take decided exception, sir. I promised a petrified reptile; I have produced one. Nine hundred and ninety-nine out of every thousand people who have ever touched a gold-mine will bear evidence to the correctness of calling it a reptile. Yes, a bloodthirsty reptile. You take things too literal, sir. If a man were to mention 'log' to you you would demand a saw-log, whereas the man might well be alluding to a ship's log."

"Ye-e-es; that's all very true, but——"

"Sir Silas, let me own up to deception. To profit by this dis-covery I was obliged to interest a capitalist. For reasons you will soon understand I wished to accomplish this without waste of time, and, having pitched upon you, I used what proved to be the best, perhaps the only, way of interesting you. You did become interested?"

"I certainly did."

"More than that, I say you are still interested, deeply inter-ested, although in a different way."

"Yes; I admit I am."

"Then I have accomplished my purpose."

"I have read you to the end, I suppose?"

"No, there are a few paragraphs more."

The millionaire recognised that beneath his feet was wealth untold, yet he was conscious of bitter disappointment. He had rather have found a fossil than a gold-mine. Nevertheless, it was a wonderful find, and his agile brain was already hard at work to devise plans for profiting from the find to the full. The two strolled back to where the guides had smudges smoking, although the flies were now few. They sat down. After a long silence Sir Silas glanced up and said: "By the way, we have seen nothing of your friend!"

"He is over there."

"Where?" Sir Silas glanced round. "I do not see him."

"There. Up yonder."

"What!" gasped the millionaire, as his eyes fell upon a cairn of stones that rose on the bank by the brink of the falls. "What! Dead?"

"Dead," answered the man in moccasins, smiling.

"You—you did not tell me that."

"I told you we exchanged shots. Mine killed."

"Heavens! Murdered?"

"Not murdered—killed."

"For the gold?"

"Again no. Not for the gold, Sir Silas, but from the weariness and misery, the bitter, gnawing loneliness, the savagery, the malevolence of the spirit of this glorious, infernal wilderness. Our souls were possessed of devils, our brains afire with gloom. We drew simultaneously. His shot scored me next the heart. Mine killed. He had the luck."

Sir Silas Martin gazed in awe at the earnest face of the man in moccasins, who, on his part, confronted the millionaire frank-faced as a sunflower.

After a space of time the Englishman drew forth a large envelope from under his blue shirt and took from it a printed form. He handed it over. It was the Government titles for the mining rights to the land on which they sat, made out in favour of a widow, a learned society, and a millionaire knight. "Ann Grace Fullerton?" queried the knight.

"His widow." The man in moccasins jerked his head towards the grave. "I found her letters in his pocket. She'll need all the good fortune that may befall her, I fancy."

Sir Silas again glanced through the document.

"Where do you come in?" he asked.

The man in moccasins rose to his feet.

"I don't come in. I go out. Sir Silas, you are rich enough to be honest. Treat the widow and the society fair and above-board. They have been notified of their possessions, but I recognise in you the leading spirit in this the Plesiosaurus Mine. It is rich enough for three. Be honest."

From the belt that girdled him the man in moccasins plucked, one by one, the cartridges of his heavy revolver and tossed them into the pool. The last of these gone, he turned abruptly and strode up the incline until he stood before the grave of his comrade. Sir Silas leapt to his feet to follow, but his muscles grew suddenly rigid when he beheld the man in moccasins take off his hat and with the other hand draw the revolver from its holster. The millionaire would have shouted, but his voice refused to come. The Indians stood stoically staring. The man in moccasins slowly raised the revolver up, and up, and up, until it was held at arm's length high above his head, its muzzle pointing to the clouds. Then the shots, one by one, each separated from the other by an impressive interval, rang out on the air. Sir Silas Martin snatched off his hat. The man in moccasins was firing a farewell volley over the grave of his friend.

Six shots delivered, the man stood for a few minutes gazing at the grave of his friend; then, turning, he leapt into the air, and with all his might flung the revolver hurtling, so that it splashed far out into the river. Replacing his hat on his head, he walked slowly towards the knight, who now sat in a state of semi-collapse on the turf. Passing the Indians he ordered, "Launch my canoe." Stepping up to Sir Silas, he held out his hand.

"I'm off," he said.

"Wh-wh-where are you off to?" stammered the trembling millionaire.

"There." He flung his hand towards Labrador. "There, and for ever. It may be my fate to live for many days, but no white man shall see my face again. I am a short story, but the end will be withheld from all but myself. Now, good-bye, Sir Silas, and—deal honestly by the widow."

He caught up his dog and squatted in the canoe. The Indians danced it across the angry stream to the far shore. He tossed the dog ashore, took his bow and arrows in his hand, and, stepping out close to the great birch tree that he had drawn so well, he scrambled up to the top of the bank. Taking off his slouch hat, he stood for some moments gazing across at Sir Silas as though loth to tear himself away; then, waving an abrupt farewell, turned round and plunged into the thicket. And that was the last ever seen or heard of the man in moccasins.

Arthur Conan Doyle

The Terror of Blue John Gap

The passion for paleontology that led ARTHUR CONAN DOYLE *(1859-1930) to write* The Lost World *(1912) stemmed from his fascination with scientific detection. Even Sherlock Holmes compares his famous deductive reasoning to the skill that had—in popular myth—enabled pioneering anatomist Georges Cuvier to reconstruct an entire extinct animal from just a single fossil.*[1] *It was only in May 1909, however, when Conan Doyle unearthed footprints of the dinosaur* Iguanodon *not far from his house in Crowborough, East Sussex, that he seems to have been inspired to bring paleontology to the focus of his fiction. While* The Lost World *would be set at the South American outposts of empire, "The Terror of Blue John Gap" brought the dangers of the prehistoric world into territory far more familiar to most of his readership. Set in the Midlands county of Derbyshire, this story was published in the August 1910 edition of the* Strand Magazine, *Conan Doyle's usual literary venue.*

THE following narrative was found among the papers of Dr. James Hardcastle, who died of phthisis on February 4th, 1908, at 36, Upper Coventry Flats, South Kensington. Those who knew him best, while refusing to express an opinion upon this particular statement, are unanimous in asserting that he was a man of a sober and scientific turn of mind, absolutely devoid of

1 Gowan Dawson, *Show Me the Bone: Reconstructing Prehistoric Monsters in Nineteenth-Century Britain and America* (Chicago: University of Chicago Press, 2016), 358-362.

imagination, and most unlikely to invent any abnormal series of events. The paper was contained in an envelope, which was docketed, "A Short Account of the Circumstances which Occurred near Miss Allerton's Farm in North-West Derbyshire in the Spring of Last Year." The envelope was sealed, and on the other side was written in pencil:—

DEAR SEATON,—It may interest, and perhaps pain, you to know that the incredulity with which you met my story has prevented me from ever opening my mouth upon the subject again. I leave this record after my death, and perhaps strangers may be found to have more confidence in me than my friend.

Inquiry has failed to elicit who this Seaton may have been. I may add that the visit of the deceased to Allerton's Farm, and the general nature of the alarm there, apart from his particular explanation, have been absolutely established. With this foreword I append his account exactly as he left it. It is in the form of a diary, some entries in which have been expanded, while a few have been erased.

April 17th.—Already I feel the benefit of this wonderful upland air. The farm of the Allertons lies fourteen hundred and twenty feet above sea-level, so it may well be a bracing climate. Beyond the usual morning cough I have very little discomfort, and, what with the fresh milk and the home-grown mutton, I have every chance of putting on weight. I think Saunderson will be pleased.

The two Miss Allertons are charmingly quaint and kind, two dear little hard-working old maids, who are ready to lavish all the heart which might have gone out to husband and to children upon an invalid stranger. Truly, the old maid is a most useful person, one of the reserve forces of the community. They talk of the superfluous woman, but what would the poor superfluous man do without her kindly presence? By the way, in their simplicity they very quickly let out the reason why Saunderson recommended their farm. The Professor rose from the ranks himself, and I believe that in his youth he was not above scaring crows in these very fields.

It is a most lonely spot, and the walks are picturesque in the extreme. The farm consists of grazing land lying at the bottom of an irregular valley. On each side are the fantastic limestone hills, formed of rock so soft that you can break it away with your hands. All this country is hollow. Could you strike it with some gigantic hammer it would boom like a drum, or possibly cave in altogether and expose some huge subterranean sea. A great sea there must surely be, for on all sides the streams run into the mountain itself, never to reappear. There are gaps everywhere amid the rocks, and when you pass through them you find yourself in great caverns, which wind down into the bowels of the earth. I have a small bicycle lamp, and it is a perpetual joy to me to carry it into these weird solitudes, and to see the wonderful silver and black effects when I throw its light upon the stalactites which drape the lofty roofs. Shut off the lamp, and you are in the blackest darkness. Turn it on, and it is a scene from the Arabian Nights.

But there is one of these strange openings in the earth which has a special interest, for it is the handiwork, not of Nature, but of Man. I had never heard of Blue John when I came to these parts. It is the name given to a peculiar mineral of a beautiful purplish shade, which is only found at one or two places in the world. It is so rare that an ordinary vase of Blue John would be valued at a great price. The Romans, with that extraordinary instinct of theirs, discovered that it was to be found in this valley, and sank a horizontal shaft deep into the mountain side. The opening of their mine has been called Blue John Gap, a clean-cut arch in the rock, the mouth all overgrown with bushes. It is a goodly passage which the Roman miners have cut, and it intersects some of the great water-worn caves, so that if you enter Blue John Gap you would do well to mark your steps and to have a good store of candles, or you may never make your way back to the daylight again. I have not yet gone deeply into it, but this very day I stood at the mouth of the arched tunnel, and peering down into the black recesses beyond I vowed that when my health returned I would devote some holiday to exploring those mysterious depths and finding out for myself how far the Romans had penetrated into the Derbyshire hills.

Strange how superstitious these countrymen are! I should have thought better of young Armitage, for he is a man of some education and character, and a very fine fellow for his station in life. I was standing at the Blue John Gap when he came across the field to me.

"Well, doctor," said he, "you're not afraid, anyhow."

"Afraid!" I answered. "Afraid of what?"

"Of It," said he, with a jerk of his thumb towards the black vault; "of the Terror that lives in the Blue John Cave."

How absurdly easy it is for a legend to arise in a lonely countryside! I examined him as to the reasons for his weird belief. It seems that from time to time sheep have been missing from the fields, carried bodily away, according to Armitage. That they could have wandered away of their own accord and disappeared among the mountains was an explanation to which he would not listen. On one occasion a pool of blood had been found, and some tufts of wool. That also, I pointed out, could be explained in a perfectly natural way. Further, the nights upon which sheep disappeared were invariably very dark, cloudy nights, with no moon. This I met with the obvious retort that those were the nights which a commonplace sheep-stealer would naturally choose for his work. On one occasion a gap had been made in a wall, and some of the stones scattered for a considerable distance. Human agency again, in my opinion.

Finally, Armitage clinched all his arguments by telling me that he had actually heard the Creature—indeed, that anyone could hear it who remained long enough at the Gap. It was a distant roaring of an immense volume. I could not but smile at this, knowing, as I do, the strange reverberations which come out of an underground water system running amid the chasms of a limestone formation. My incredulity annoyed Armitage, so that he turned and left me with some abruptness.

And now comes the queer point about the whole business. I was still standing near the mouth of the cave, turning over in my mind the various statements of Armitage and reflecting how readily they could be explained away, when suddenly, from the depth of the tunnel beside me, there issued a most extraordinary sound. How shall I describe it? First of all, it seemed to be a great distance away, far down in the bowels of the earth. Secondly, in spite of this suggestion of distance, it was very loud. Lastly, it was not a boom, nor a crash, such as one would associate with falling water or tumbling rock; but it was a high whine, tremulous and vibrating, almost like the whinnying of a horse. It was certainly a most remarkable experience, and one which for a moment, I must admit, gave a new significance to Armitage's words. I waited by the Blue John Gap for half an hour or more, but there was no return of the sound, so at last I wandered back to the farm-house, rather mystified by what had occurred. Decidedly I shall explore that cavern when my strength is restored. Of course, Armitage's explanation is too absurd for discussion, and yet that sound was certainly very strange. It still rings in my ears as I write.

April 20th.—In the last three days I have made several expeditions to the Blue John Gap, and have even penetrated some short distance, but my bicycle lantern is so small and weak that I dare not trust myself very far. I shall do the thing more systematically. I have heard no sound at all, and could almost believe that I had been the victim of some hallucination suggested, perhaps, by Armitage's conversation. Of course, the whole idea is absurd, and yet I must confess that those bushes at the entrance of the cave do present an appearance as if some heavy creature had forced its way through them. I begin to be keenly interested. I have said nothing to the Miss Allertons, for they are quite superstitious enough already, but I have bought some candles, and mean to investigate for myself.

I observed this morning that among the numerous tufts of sheep's wool which lay among the bushes near the cavern there was one which was smeared with blood. Of course, my reason tells me that if sheep wander into such rocky places they are likely to injure themselves, and yet somehow that splash of crimson gave me a sudden shock, and for a moment I found myself shrinking back in horror from the old Roman arch. A fetid breath seemed to ooze from the black depths into which I peered. Could it indeed be possible that some nameless thing, some dreadful presence, was lurking down yonder? I should have been incapable of such feelings in the days of my strength, but one grows more nervous and fanciful when one's health is shaken.

For the moment I weakened in my resolution, and was ready to leave the secret of the old mine, if one exists, for ever unsolved. But to-night my interest has returned and my nerves grown more steady. To-morrow I trust that I shall have gone more deeply into this matter.

April 22nd.—Let me try and set down as accurately as I can my extraordinary experience of yesterday. I started in the afternoon, and made my way to the Blue John Gap. I confess that my misgivings returned as I gazed into its depths, and I wished that I had brought a companion to share my exploration. Finally, with a return of resolution, I lit my candle, pushed my way through the briers, and descended into the rocky shaft.

It went down at an acute angle for some fifty feet, the floor being covered with broken stone. Thence there extended a long, straight passage cut in the solid rock. I am no geologist, but the lining of this corridor was certainly of some harder material than limestone, for there were points where I could actually see the tool-marks which the old miners had left in their excavation, as fresh as if they had been done yesterday. Down this strange, old-world corridor I stumbled, my feeble flame throwing a dim circle of light around me, which made the shadows beyond the more threatening and obscure. Finally, I came to a spot where the Roman tunnel opened into a water-worn cavern—a huge hall, hung with long white icicles of lime deposit. From this central chamber I could dimly perceive that a number of passages worn by the subterranean streams wound away into the depths of the earth. I was standing there wondering whether I had better return, or whether I dare venture farther into this dangerous labyrinth, when my eyes fell upon something at my feet which strongly arrested my attention.

The greater part of the floor of the cavern was covered with boulders of rock or with hard incrustations of lime; but at this particular point there had been a drip from the distant roof, which had left a patch of soft mud. In the very centre of this there was a huge mark—an ill-defined blotch, deep, broad, and irregular, as if a great boulder had fallen upon it. No loose stone lay near, however, nor was there anything to account for the impression. It was far too large to be caused by any possible animal, and, besides, there was only the one, and the patch of mud was of such a size that no reasonable stride could have covered it. As I rose from the examination of that singular mark and then looked round into the black shadows which hemmed me in, I must confess that I felt for a moment a most unpleasant sinking of my heart, and that, do what I would, the candle trembled in my outstretched hand.

I soon recovered my nerve, however, when I reflected how absurd it was to associate so huge and shapeless a mark with the track of any known animal. Even an elephant could not have produced it. I determined, therefore, that I would not be scared by vague and senseless fears from carrying out my exploration. Before proceeding I took good note of a curious rock formation in the wall by which I could recognize the entrance of the Roman tunnel. The precaution was very necessary, for the great cave, so far as I could see it, was intersected by passages. Having made sure of my position, and reassured myself by examining my spare candles and my matches, I advanced slowly over the rocky and uneven surface of the cavern.

And now I come to the point where I met with such sudden and desperate disaster. A stream, some twenty feet broad, ran across my path, and I walked for some little distance along the bank to find a spot where I could cross dryshod. Finally, I came to a place where a single flat boulder lay near the centre, which I could reach in a stride. As it chanced, however, the rock had been cut away and made top-heavy by the rush of the stream, so that it tilted over as I landed on it, and shot me into the ice-cold water. My candle went out, and I found myself floundering about in an utter and absolute darkness.

I staggered to my feet again, more amused than alarmed by my adventure. The candle had fallen from my hand, and was lost in the stream, but I had two others in my pocket, so that it was of no importance. I got one of them ready, and drew out my box of matches to light it. Only then did I realize my position. The box had been soaked in my fall into the river. It was impossible to strike the matches.

A cold hand seemed to close round my heart as I realized my position. The darkness was opaque and horrible. It was so utter that one put one's hand up to one's face as if to press off something solid. I stood still, and by an effort I steadied myself. I tried to reconstruct in my mind a map of the floor of the cavern as I had last seen it. Alas! the bearings which had impressed themselves upon my mind were high on the wall, and not to be found by touch. Still, I remembered in a general way how the sides were situated, and I hoped that by groping my way along them I would at last come to the opening of the Roman tunnel. Moving very slowly, and continually striking against the rocks, I set out on this desperate quest.

But I very soon realized how impossible it was. In that black, velvety darkness one lost all one's bearings in an instant. Before I had made a dozen paces I was utterly bewildered as to my whereabouts. The rippling of the stream, which was the one sound audible, showed me where it lay, but the moment that I left its bank I was utterly lost. The idea of finding my way back in absolute darkness through that limestone labyrinth was clearly an impossible one.

I sat down upon a boulder and reflected upon my unfortunate plight. I had not told anyone that I proposed to come to the Blue John mine, and it was unlikely that a search party would come after me. Therefore, I must trust to my own resources to get clear of the danger. There was only one hope, and that was that the matches might dry. When I fell into the river only half of me had got thoroughly wet. My left shoulder had remained above the water. I took the box of matches, therefore, and put it into my left armpit. The moist air of the cavern might possibly be counteracted by the heat of my body, but even so I knew that I could not hope to get a light for many hours. Meanwhile there was nothing for it but to wait.

By good luck I had slipped several biscuits into my pocket before I left the farm-house. These I now devoured, and washed them down with a draught from that wretched stream which had been the cause of all my misfortunes. Then I felt about for a comfortable seat among the rocks, and, having discovered a place where I could get a support for my back, I stretched out my legs and settled myself down to wait. I was wretchedly damp and cold, but I tried to cheer myself with the reflection that modern science prescribed open windows and walks in all weather for my disease. Gradually, lulled by the monotonous gurgle of the stream and by the absolute darkness, I sank into an uneasy slumber.

How long this lasted I cannot say. It may have been for one hour, it may have been for several. Suddenly I sat up on my rock couch, with every nerve thrilling and every sense acutely on the alert. Beyond all doubt I had heard a sound—some sound very distinct from the gurgling of the waters. It had passed, but the reverberation of it still lingered in my ear. Was it a search party? They would most certainly have shouted, and vague as this sound was which had wakened me, it was very distinct from the human voice. I sat palpitating and hardly daring to breathe. There it was again! And again! Now it had become continuous. It was a tread—yes, surely it was the tread of some living creature. But what a tread it was! It gave one the impression of enormous weight carried upon sponge-like feet, which gave forth a muffled but ear-filling sound. The darkness was as complete as ever, but the tread was regular and decisive. And it was coming beyond all question in my direction.

My skin grew cold, and my hair stood on end as I listened to that steady and ponderous footfall. There was some creature there, and surely, by the speed of its advance, it was one who could see in the dark. I crouched low on my rock and tried to blend myself into it. The steps grew nearer still, then stopped, and presently I was aware of a loud lapping and gurgling. The creature was drinking at the stream. Then again there was silence, broken by a succession of long sniffs and snorts, of tremendous volume and energy. Had it caught the scent of me? My own nostrils were filled by a low fetid odour, mephitic and abominable. Then I heard the steps again. They were on my side of the stream now. The stones rattled within a few yards of where I lay. Hardly daring to breathe, I crouched upon my rock. Then the steps drew away. I heard the splash as it returned across the river, and the sound died away into the distance in the direction from which it had come.

For a long time I lay upon the rock, too much horrified to move. I thought of the sound which I had heard coming from the depths of the cave, of Armitage's fears, of the strange impression in the mud, and now came this final and absolute proof that there was indeed some inconceivable monster, something utterly un-English and dreadful, which lurked in the hollow of the mountain. Of its nature or form I could frame no conception, save that it was both light-footed and gigantic. The combat between my reason, which told me that such things could not be, and my senses, which told me that they were, raged within me as I lay. Finally, I was almost ready to persuade myself that this experience had been part of some evil dream, and that my abnormal condition might have conjured up a hallucination. But there remained one final experience which removed the last possibility of doubt from my mind.

I had taken my matches from my armpit and felt them. They seemed perfectly hard and dry. Stooping down into a crevice of the rocks, I tried one of them. To my delight it took fire at once. I lit the candle, and, with a terrified backward glance into the obscure depths of the cavern, I hurried in the direction of the Roman passage. As I did so I passed the patch of mud on which I had seen the huge imprint. Now I stood astonished before it, for there were three similar imprints upon its surface, enormous in size, irregular in outline, of a depth which indicated the ponderous weight which had left them. Then a great terror surged over me. Stooping and shading my candle with my hand, I ran in a frenzy of fear to the rocky archway, hastened up it, and never stopped until, with weary feet and panting lungs, I rushed up the final slope of stones, broke through the tangle of briers, and flung myself exhausted upon the soft grass under the peaceful light of the stars. It was three in the morning when I reached the farm-house, and to-day I am all unstrung and quivering after my terrific adventure. As yet I have told no one. I must move warily in the matter. What would the poor lonely women, or the uneducated yokels here, think of it if I were to tell them my experience? Let me go to someone who can understand and advise.

April 25th.—I was laid up in bed for two days after my incredible adventure in the cavern. I use the adjective with a very definite meaning, for I have had an experience since which has shocked me almost as much as the other. I have said that I was looking round for someone who could advise me. There is a Dr. Mark Johnson who practises some few miles away, to whom I had a note of recommendation from Professor Saunderson. To him I drove, when I was strong enough to get about, and I recounted to him my whole strange experience. He listened intently, and then carefully examined me, paying special attention to my reflexes and to the pupils of my eyes. When he had finished he refused to discuss my adventure, saying that it was entirely beyond him, but he gave me the card of a Mr. Picton at Castleton, with the advice that I should instantly go to him and tell him the story exactly as I had done it to himself. He was, according to my adviser, the very man who was pre-eminently suited to help me. I went on to the station, therefore, and made my way to the little town, which is some ten miles away. Mr. Picton appeared to be a man of importance, as his brass plate was displayed upon the door of a considerable building on the outskirts of the town. I was about to ring his bell, when some misgiving came into my mind, and, crossing to a neighbouring shop, I asked the man behind the counter if he could tell me anything of Mr. Picton. "Why," said he, "he is the best mad doctor in Derbyshire, and yonder is his asylum." You can imagine that it was not long before I had shaken the dust of Castleton from my feet and returned to the farm, cursing all unimaginative pedants who cannot conceive that there may be things in creation which have never yet chanced to come across their mole's vision. After all, now that I am cooler, I can afford to admit that I have been no more sympathetic to Armitage than Dr. Johnson has been to me.

April 27th.—When I was a student I had the reputation of being a man of courage and enterprise. I remember that when there was a ghost-hunt at Coltbridge it was I who sat up in the haunted house. Is it advancing years (after all, I am only thirty-five), or is it this physical malady which has caused degeneration? Certainly my heart quails when I think of that horrible cavern in the hill, and the certainty that it has some monstrous occupant. What shall I do? There is not an hour in the day that I do not debate the question. If I say nothing, then the mystery remains unsolved. If I do say anything, then I have the alternative of mad alarm over the whole countryside, or of absolute incredulity which may end in consigning me to an asylum. On the whole, I think that my best course is to wait, and to prepare for some expedition which shall be more deliberate and better thought-out than the last. As a first step I have been to Castleton and obtained a few essentials—a large acetylene lantern for one thing, and a good double-barrelled sporting rifle for another. The latter I have hired, but I have bought a dozen heavy game cartridges, which would bring down a rhinoceros. Now I am ready for my troglodyte friend. Give me better health and a little spate of energy, and I shall try conclusions with him yet. But who and what is he? Ah! there is the question which stands between me and my sleep. How many theories do I form, only to discard each in turn! It is all so utterly unthinkable. And yet the cry, the footmark, the tread in the cavern—no reasoning can get past these. I think of the old-world legends of dragons and of other monsters. Were they, perhaps, not such fairy-tales as we have thought? Can it be that there is some fact which underlies them, and am I, of all mortals, the one who is chosen to expose it?

May 3rd.—For several days I have been laid up by the vagaries of an English spring, and during those days there have been developments, the true and sinister meaning of which no one can appreciate save myself. I may say that we have had cloudy and moonless nights of late, which according to my information were the seasons upon which sheep disappeared. Well, sheep *have* disappeared. Two of Miss Allerton's, one of old Pearson's of the Cat Walk, and one of Mrs. Moulton's. Four in all, during three nights. No trace is left of them at all, and the countryside is buzzing with rumours of gipsies and of sheep-stealers.

But there is something more serious than that. Young Armitage has disappeared also. He left his moorland cottage early on Wednesday night, and has never been heard of since. He was an unattached man, so there is less sensation than would otherwise be the case. The popular explanation is that he owes money, and has found a situation in some other part of the country, whence he will presently write for his belongings. But I have grave misgivings. Is it not much more likely that the recent tragedy of the sheep has caused him to take some steps which may have ended in his own destruction? He may, for example, have lain in wait for the creature, and been carried off by it into the recesses of the mountains. What an inconceivable fate for a civilized Englishman of the twentieth century! And yet I feel that it is possible and even probable. But in that case, how far am I answerable both for his death and for any other mishap which may occur? Surely with the knowledge I already possess it must be my duty to see that something is done, or if necessary to do it myself. It must be the latter, for this morning I went down to the local police-station and told my story. The inspector entered it all in a large book and bowed me out with commendable gravity, but I heard a burst of laughter before I had got down his garden path. No doubt he was recounting my adventure to his family.

June 10th.——I am writing this, propped up in bed, six weeks after my last entry in this journal. I have gone through a terrible shock both to mind and body, arising from such an experience as has seldom befallen a human being before. But I have attained my end. The danger from the Terror which dwells in the Blue John Gap has passed, never to return. Thus much at least I, a broken invalid, have done for the common good. Let me now recount what occurred as clearly as I may.

The night of Friday, May 3rd, was dark and cloudy—the very night for the monster to walk. About eleven o'clock I went from the farm-house with my lantern and my rifle, having first left a note upon the table of my bedroom in which I said that if I were missing search should be made for me in the direction of the Gap. I made my way to the mouth of the Roman shaft, and, having perched myself among the rocks close to the opening, I shut off my lantern and waited patiently with my loaded rifle ready to my hand.

It was a melancholy vigil. All down the winding valley I could see the scattered lights of the farm-houses, and the church clock of Chapel-le-Dale tolling the hours, came faintly to my ears. These tokens of my fellow-men served only to make my own position seem the more lonely, and to call for a greater effort to overcome the terror which tempted me continually to get back to the farm, and abandon for ever this dangerous quest. And yet there lies deep in every man a rooted self-respect which makes it hard for him to turn back from that which he has once undertaken. This feeling of personal pride was my salvation now, and it was that alone which held me fast when every instinct of my nature was dragging me away. I am glad now that I had the strength. In spite of all that it has cost me, my manhood is at least above reproach.

Twelve o'clock struck in the distant church, then one, then two. It was the darkest hour of the night. The clouds were drifting low, and there was not a star in the sky. An owl was hooting somewhere among the rocks, but no other sound, save the gentle sough of the wind, came to my ears. And then suddenly I heard it! From far away down the tunnel came those muffled steps, so soft and yet so ponderous. I heard also the rattle of stones as they gave way under that giant tread. They drew nearer. They were close upon me. I heard the crashing of the bushes round the entrance, and then dimly through the darkness I was conscious of the loom of some enormous shape, some monstrous inchoate creature, passing swiftly and very silently out from the tunnel. I was paralyzed with fear and amazement. Long as I had waited, now that it had actually come I was unprepared for the shock. I lay motionless and breathless, whilst the great dark mass whisked by me and was swallowed up in the night.

But now I nerved myself for its return. No sound came from the sleeping countryside to tell of the horror which was loose. In no way could I judge how far off it was, what it was doing, or when it might be back. But not a second time should my nerve fail me, not a second time should it pass unchallenged. I swore it between my clenched teeth as I laid my cocked rifle across the rock.

And yet it nearly happened. There was no warning of approach now as the creature passed over the grass. Suddenly, like a dark, drifting shadow, the huge bulk loomed up once more before me, making for the entrance of the cave. Again came that paralysis of volition, which held my crooked forefinger impotent upon the trigger. But with a desperate effort I shook it off. Even as the brushwood rustled, and the monstrous beast blended with the shadow of the Gap, I fired at the retreating form. In the blaze of the gun I caught a glimpse of a great shaggy mass, something with rough and bristling hair of a withered grey colour, fading away to white in its lower parts, the huge body supported upon short, thick, curving legs. I had just that glance, and then I heard the rattle of the stones as the creature tore down into its burrow. In an instant, with a triumphant revulsion of feeling, I had cast my fears to the wind, and uncovering my powerful lantern, with my rifle in my hand, I sprang down from my rock and rushed after the monster down the old Roman shaft.

My splendid lamp cast a brilliant flood of vivid light in front of me, very different from the yellow glimmer which had aided me down the same passage only twelve days before. As I ran I saw the great beast lurching along before me, its huge bulk filling up the whole space from wall to wall. Its hair looked like coarse faded oakum, and hung down in long, dense masses which swayed as it moved. It was like an enormous unclipped sheep in its fleece, but in size it was far larger than the largest elephant, and its breadth seemed to be nearly as great as its height. It fills me with amazement now to think that I should have dared to follow such a horror into the bowels of the earth, but when one's blood is up, and when one's quarry seems to be flying, the old primeval hunting spirit awakes and prudence is cast to the wind. Rifle in hand, I ran at the top of my speed upon the trail of the monster.

I had seen that the creature was swift. Now I was to find out to my cost that it was also very cunning. I had imagined that it was in panic flight, and that I had only to pursue it. The idea that it might turn upon me never entered my excited brain. I have already explained that the passage down which I was racing opened into a great central cave. Into this I rushed, fearful lest I should lose all trace of the beast. But he had turned upon his own traces, and in a moment we were face to face.

That picture, seen in the brilliant white light of the lantern, is etched for ever upon my brain. He had reared up on his hind legs as a bear would do, and stood above me, enormous, menacing—such a creature as no nightmare had ever brought to my imagination. I have said that he reared like a bear, and there was something bear-like—if one could conceive a bear which was tenfold the bulk of any bear seen upon earth—in his whole pose and attitude, in his great crooked forelegs with their ivory-white claws, in his rugged skin, and in his red, gaping mouth, fringed with monstrous fangs. Only in one point did he differ from the bear, or from any other creature which walks the earth, and even at that supreme moment a shudder of horror passed over me as I observed that the eyes which glistened in the glow of my lantern were huge, projecting bulbs, white and sightless. For a moment his great paws swung over my head. The next he fell forward upon me, I and my broken lantern crashed to the earth, and I remember no more.

When I came to myself I was back in the farm-house of the Allertons. Two days had passed since my terrible adventure in the Blue John Gap. It seems that I had lain all night in the cave insensible from concussion of the brain, with my left arm and two ribs badly fractured. In the morning my note had been found, a search party of a dozen farmers assembled, and I had been tracked down and carried back to my bedroom, where I had lain in high delirium ever since. There was, it seems, no sign of the creature, and no bloodstain which would show that my bullet had found him as he passed. Save for my own plight and the marks upon the mud, there was nothing to prove that what I said was true.

Six weeks have now elapsed, and I am able to sit out once more in the sunshine. Just opposite me is the steep hillside, grey with shaly rock, and yonder on its flank is the dark cleft which marks the opening of the Blue John Gap. But it is no longer a source of terror. Never again through that ill-omened tunnel shall any strange shape flit out into the world of men. The educated and the scientific, the Dr. Johnsons and the like, may smile at my narrative, but the poorer folk of the countryside had never a doubt as to its truth. On the day after my recovering consciousness they assembled in their hundreds round the Blue John Gap. As the *Castleton Courier* said:—

"It was useless for our correspondent, or for any of the

adventurous gentlemen who had come from Matlock, Buxton, and other parts, to offer to descend, to explore the cave to the end, and to finally test the extraordinary narrative of Dr. James Hardcastle. The country people had taken the matter into their own hands, and from an early hour of the morning they had worked hard in stopping up the entrance of the tunnel. There is a sharp slope where the shaft begins, and great boulders, rolled along by many willing hands, were thrust down it until the Gap was absolutely sealed. So ends the episode which has caused such excitement throughout the country. Local opinion is fiercely divided upon the subject. On the one hand are those who point to Dr. Hardcastle's impaired health, and to the possibility of cerebral lesions of tubercular origin giving rise to strange hallucinations. Some *idée fixe*, according to these gentlemen, caused the doctor to wander down the tunnel, and a fall among the rocks was sufficient to account for his injuries. On the other hand, a legend of a strange creature in the Gap has existed for some months back, and the farmers look upon Dr. Hardcastle's narrative and his personal injuries as a final corroboration. So the matter stands, and so the matter will continue to stand, for no definite solution seems to us to be now possible. It transcends human wit to give any scientific explanation which could cover the alleged facts."

Perhaps before the *Courier* published these words they would have been wise to send their representative to me. I have thought the matter out, as no one else has had occasion to do, and it is possible that I might have removed some of the more obvious difficulties of the narrative and brought it one degree nearer to scientific acceptance. Let me then write down the only explanation which seems to me to elucidate what I know to my cost to have been a series of facts. My theory may seem to be wildly improbable, but at least no one can venture to say that it is impossible.

My view is—and it was formed, as is shown by my diary,

before my personal adventure—that in this part of England there is a vast subterranean lake or sea, which is fed by the great number of streams which pass down through the limestone. Where there is a large collection of water there must also be some evaporation, mists or rain, and a possibility of vegetation. This in turn suggests that there may be animal life, arising, as the vegetable life would also do, from those seeds and types which had been introduced at an early period of the world's history, when communication with the outer air was more easy. This place had then developed a fauna and flora of its own, including such monsters as the one which I had seen, which may well have been the old cave bear, enormously enlarged and modified by its new environment. For countless æons the internal and the external creation had kept apart, growing steadily away from each other. Then there had come some rift in the depths of the mountain which had enabled one creature to wander up and, by means of the Roman tunnel, to reach the open air. Like all subterranean life, it had lost the power of sight, but this had no doubt been compensated for by Nature in other directions. Certainly it had some means of finding its way about, and of hunting down the sheep upon the hillside. As to its choice of dark nights, it is part of my theory that light was painful to those great white eyeballs, and that it was only a pitch-black world which it could tolerate. Perhaps, indeed, it was the glare of my lantern which saved my life at that awful moment when we were face to face. So I read the riddle. I leave these facts behind me, and if you can explain them, do so; or if you choose to doubt them, do so. Neither your belief nor your incredulity can alter them, nor affect one whose task is nearly over.

So ended the strange narrative of Dr. James Hardcastle.

Theodore Dru Alison Cockerell

Progress: A Drama of Evolution

The horrors of the Great War seemed a dramatic rebuttal to the West's notions of its own general progress—notions which had been reinforced by the apparently progressive nature of the paleontological record. Fossils appeared to tell an upward story from the simple organisms of life's dawn to the intellectual civilization of modern humanity. The technical nuances of this story were familiar to Anglo-American zoologist and paleontologist Theodore Dru Alison Cockerell (1866-1948), *a professor at the University of Colorado. This March 1916 contribution to the American Museum of Natural History's magazine, the* American Museum Journal, *takes a closer look at what "progress" has constituted throughout geohistory. Cockerell, who was interested in the power of poetry, chose to make his point in a closet verse drama. Its characters—namely anthropomorphic invertebrates, amphibians, dinosaurs, early mammals, birds, and primitive humans—argue over evolution and ethics in consciously archaic stylings. The drama culminates in a timely clash between Peace and War. "I am by no means sure," reflected Cockerell two decades later, "that this play, suitably modified for presentation, would not be effective on the stage or on the screen."*[1]

Argument.—Evolutionary progress has not flowed in a single continuous stream from amœba to man; it has branched and branched again, so that the ramifications are more numerous than the mind can follow. The most significant new branches

[1] Theodore Dru Alison Cockerell, "Recollections of a Naturalist, IX. Verse," *Bios*, 9 (1938), 66-70 (69).

have not arisen from the ends of the old ones, but as entirely new departures from the main trunk of the tree. Thus each great innovation, full of meaning for the future, has at first appeared to contradict the teachings of the past. The new types have usually been feeble and insignificant, never robust and dominant; and if we permit ourselves to imagine an attitude of the other creatures toward them, it must be one of contempt. In the first act, the forerunners of the vertebrates are represented by the modern Prochordates, to enable us to visualize the types, although the actual actors in the drama are of course extinct and unknown. For similar reasons, the invertebrates are represented by living species. The adoption of a new position, whereby the main nerve cord is dorsal, contradicts all invertebrate usage from the earliest times; the notochord is an entirely new development. In the course of development, the tunicate loses all the characters suggesting an approach to the vertebrate types and becomes a degenerate, sedentary sac. The *Balanoglossus* resembles a worm; but the *Amphioxus* retains its fishlike form, its well-developed nerve cord and notochord.

The vertebrate type having duly developed in the water, the second act records the discovery of the land by some primitive amphibian, here personified by the frog. The frog celebrates his passover every spring; no wonder he sings aloud in the marshes! The ability to live on land opened up a great new field for growth and development, with the accompanying modification of the paired fins into digitate limbs, the fundamental change of structure making possible all future progress.

The vertebrate type on land developed into mighty but cold-blooded beasts, such as the giant *Diplodocus*, named after Mr. Carnegie, to be seen in the Carnegie Museum, Pittsburgh, and in the American Museum. These vast dinosaurs were contemporaneous with early forms of mammals, small but warm-blooded. In time the great reptiles perished, and the mammals came to their own.

After a long course of mammalian evolution, a creature appeared, erect upon its hinder legs, with hands free to use tools. Much earlier, the birds had ceased to walk upon the anterior limbs, but had missed the possibility of human-like change through developing wings. Now comes man, relatively feeble, ugly from the standpoint of the other animals (even we regard with disgust a hairless Mexican dog), apparently a sort of developmental joke, but destined to become the topmost branch of the evolutionary tree. Conscious of his own weakness, he nevertheless puts on a bold front.

In these modern days, teachers, professing to hold the learning of the past, are telling us that we "cannot change human nature"; that every wicked and vicious thing has its roots in nature, and however much it is to be deplored, it must be endured. This attitude is one of the deep fundamental causes of the present war. Let us learn indeed from the past, that significant progress is always possible, but through narrow paths, which to our eyes, blinded by the light of custom, seem dark and dangerous. Hazarding these byways, many of us must fail, but the few who succeed will win for the human race the rich prizes of the future. This is not mere sentiment; it is the teaching of science and of universal experience.

Act I

Beneath the waters of the ocean. Seaweeds, lobsters,
crabs, mollusks, etc.

Time, Late Cambrian

Enter AMPHIOXUS, LARVAL TUNICATE *and* BALANOGLOSSUS

AMPHIOXUS. We are not much to look at, but we are
All in the way of progress.

Our backs are stiffened by a notochord, and all above
A slender nerve cord runs from fore to aft,
Prophetic of a brain. This tiny spot, this little speck of black,
Will some day be a pair of eyes, to knowingly survey the world,
While these gill slits, ranged on each side, already serve
To liven us with oxygen, gleaned from the waters flowing
    through them.
All in the way of progress to be vertebrates, and in the days to come
Perchance, some creature with a soul.

LOBSTER. All in the way of progress! Are you mad?
I tell you, sirs, the progress of the past has not been thus.
In years so many that to count by millions is fatiguing,
In all the ages since the Cambrian dawn, and all the unknown
    times before
Was never such a thing.
Your nerve cord dorsal! Do you know
You're upside down? Clean topsy-turvy, and this somersault
You say is progress! You think the learning of the past
Is nothing. The spirit of creation, giving lobsters, crabs and snails,
Fine worms, starfishes and sea cucumbers: all this
Can now be set at naught, and you, clean upside down,
Will lead the van of progress!

[*All the animals laugh inordinately.*]

OYSTER. Our good crustaceous friend speaks truly; let me ask
Where would your progress take you?
What is a vertebrate, and what this thing
You say might have a soul?
No science teaches of such things, nor any story of the past;
A crab we know, a shrimp we know, a limpet is concrete and real,
But this absurdity you tell of, what is it?
A recollection of a dream that dreamed of dreams,

A twist of thought so meaningless that it is less than nothing.
Come friends, forsake your quest and be like us!

SEA URCHIN. Moreover, just consider how you look:
Small, soft and pallid or mud-colored.
No legs, no spines, no shell, no gaudy hues
To make you seem in fashion, and in form
To mix in good society.
In truth there's nothing in your favour save the claim
That you mean progress, and that notion's so absurd
It serves but to condemn you.

TUNICATE. Alas! What have we come to
In this mad quest for progress?
I fear 'tis as our friends declare, we're topsy-turvy,
And in seeking what is not, have lost what is.
For me no hope of excellence is left, no hope of being fit to stand
With lobster, snail or maritime cucumber. Yet I may show
My penitence in just one way, I may forego
These modern airs and change into a humble squirting sac.

BALANOGLOSSUS. And I also must hide my new conceits,
And simulate a worm. I pray you friends,
In charity pretend I am a worm.

AMPHIOXUS. Oh, comrades of such slender faith,
O'ercome by tory talk,
No future lies in store for you
But one dull round to walk.
Invertebrates you cannot be,
Nor vertebrates withal,
Alone among the beasts of sea,
The laughing stock of all.
My children are the heirs of time,

My sons will rule the earth,
When vertebrates come to their own,
And human things have birth.

Act II

In the depths of a shady pool. FROGS *and* FISHES

FIRST SCENE

FROG. Long have I lived in deep pellucid pools.
Life has been sweet among the tangled weeds.
Food has been cheap, since here Dame Nature breeds
Abundantly her water worms, while schools
Of little fishes serve our utmost needs.
And yet, in midst of plenty, discontent
Arose, and urged by some strange sprite,
I must be going upward to the light,
Toward the upper air with full intent
To face the sun, and see the stars by night.

FISH. By all my barbels, 'tis a crazy thought,
What frenzy has possessed you? Do you know
This air you talk of is not fit for use
By vertebrated beasts, gilled and soft-skinned,
Or clothed in scaly armor. The insect host, all chitin-clad
May live on earth in air, as may the plants that raise their fronds
O'er marsh and pool. But as for us,
The highest of created things, we need the best environment,
The flowing waves, soft sand and mud,
Where heat and dryness, cold and wind,
Do not beset us.

FROG. Yet I must go, and do believe
'Tis in the way of progress.
Why else am I possessed of limbs,
With jointed toes and power to jump?

FISH. Jump back into the water!

FROG. No, jump on land, and see the sights
No vertebrate has seen before.
Go up and down, and eat the lowly things
Which heretofore have gone scot-free,
Except they ate each other.
Broad is the world and wide the great expanse
Of land whereon the highest life may flourish,
Where oxygen is plenty and warm rays
Of sun above will make us grow apace.

[*Crawls out on to the land and disappears from view*.]

SECOND SCENE

In the same pool. The FISHES *discuss*

FIRST FISH. Where is our frog? I heard him talk
Of sun and air, and things above—can he have left us?
Would he risk his life on land?

SECOND FISH. Indeed he would, and has. Ah! foolish frog,
Thinking the pool not good enough he must go forth
And roam upon the land. 'Twas ever thus
Since world began. Thus is creation stultified
By its creations. Making life to fit the world whereon we live,
Toiling toward perfection, gaining a certain goal,
Only to see its beings burst their bounds, reject the past,

And seek at peril of their lives some other thing.

FIRST FISH. I do believe in progress; in the past
Seeking through wholesome change a worthy end.
It was not ill that vertebrate was born,
Lowly and humble, upside down, despised of all,
So came our founder to the world.
Think of it, friend! and speak not ill of progress.

SECOND FISH. So you support the frog in his desires
And think we all should seek the land?

FIRST FISH. Support the frog! I said not so!
All I support is progress:
Liberal at heart I love the word,
But not the actions of the frog.
All progress has an aim, and I can see
How all the past conspired to reach an end,
Through toil and conflict up and down the world,
Age upon age, was yet one purpose clear,
To make a fish.

SECOND FISH. This fish now made, what need of further progress?

FIRST FISH. This fish now made, creation's task is done:
Bright scales and fins, sharp teeth, and eyes to see
Our prey. Perfect we are, and perfect must remain,
Scorning all change. Yet since we came
To what we are through progress, we must love
The abstract thought of progress, and believe
'Tis still a blesséd word.

SECOND FISH. Blesséd for what?

FIRST FISH. Blesséd for what? Oh foolish fish!
It is not what we do, but what we think
That makes us blesséd! For what we think
We are; and if for reasons of our own
Our actions do belie our inmost thoughts,
Those thoughts still make us blesséd.
Thus may we keep the truth that helped the past,
Yet do the deeds that serve us in our day.

[*The fishes swim away together.*]

Act III

A Mesozoic Forest. DINOSAURS *and* PRIMITIVE MAMMALS

DIPLODOCUS. Help, help!—Nay, nay, there's naught amiss,
I was but dreaming, and did call for help
Forgetting that I was the lord of all creation.
For as I dreamed I seemed to lose my flesh
And stand stark naked in my giant bones.
And then, this horrid semblance of the thing I was
Appeared to find a place in some great hall,
Appeared to have a label and a name—
A name I know not, dedicating my great self
To some mammalian biped!
The thing's absurd, and yet I am obsessed
With vile forebodings, connecting these small beasts,
These mammals running in and out beneath our feet,
With evil in the days to come.

BRONTOSAURUS. Since you have said it, I will now confess
To like forebodings; though that dream of yours
Looks scarcely forward in the stream of time,

But rightly judged tells rather of the past,
The recent past when you had dined too well.

DIPLODOCUS. Can I believe it? Nay I dined too ill,
For in the marshes where I get my food
These frisky vermin have so multiplied
That food is lacking. If my dream
Has aught to do with food, it can but seem
The echo of a scanty meal.

BRONTOSAURUS. If that is so, I fear 'tis not the first,
For look you, friend, while one of us is born,
Hatched from the egg and grown to full maturity,
Nature can make a million such as these.

DIPLODOCUS. A million million vermin, and therein
Abandon all the painful gains of time!
Do we not know that progress in the past,
The dorsal nerve cord and the leap on land,
The struggle through the ages, meeting each demand
For better life, has reached its end in us?

BRONTOSAURUS. I do believe in progress; could I see
The hope of greater or of stronger beasts,
Of vaster bulk or longer neck or better tail,
Of thicker skin or armored coat of mail,
I might be then content to die and fail,
If failing made for progress.

PRIMITIVE MAMMAL. Good masters, we have heard your angry talk,
Wherein you set it forth that we may balk
The onward march of progress. Pray you halt
Your condemnation. Can it be our fault
That we are small and active, living well

The lives we have; should this foretell
The downfall of your race?

BRONTOSAURUS. But look you, little beast, your blood is warm,
Your skin is hairy, and though small you swarm
Through glade and forest.
In all the past since Cambrian dawn,
Through all the changeful weary days,
Enduring night for hopeful morn,
Was never such a craze. You do upset
The whole great scheme of progress, and forget
The lessons of the elder days.

PRIMITIVE MAMMAL. Great sir, we see in you and yours
Creation's finished work. 'Tis not for us
To emulate your greatness. Yet we would try
A line of progress all our own, and by and by
In ages yet to come evolve a man,
A being who with wingéd thought may span
The starry skies, and as in time he dies
Soar thither as a soul!

BRONT. AND DIP. [*Laughing.*] A soul! a man! So that's your plan
For further progress!

DIPLODOCUS [*Addressing Brontosaurus.*] Our fears were baseless,
        since they aim
At sky and not at earth;
Dreaming of men with wingéd thoughts
And souls to soar above!

BRONTOSAURUS. Reason failing, knowledge spurned,
Lessons of the past unlearned,
Dreaming, seeking ghosts of dreams,

Misty thought which scarcely seems
To hold a meaning.
What is there here to fright us so,
With all our strength, and since we know
We are no seeming?

Act IV

Late Tertiary. In a forest. PRIMITIVE MAN *and various animals*

HYÆNA. [*Laughing.*] Oh! have you seen, have you but seen the
    thing they call a man?
His body's out of shape and placed on end,
Erect upon his hinder legs, his hair is gone,
And hideously naked stalks he through the glade.
Creation must be crazy to have made
So foul a beast!

JACKAL. The other morn I saw some human cubs
More helpless than their sires, mere blobs of flesh,
Squirming and squealing, while with mute distress
Their mothers sought to mend their evil fate.
Feeble in youth and age, in sooth the date
Of man's extinction must be near at hand.

HYÆNA. Full well they know it, for they can but ken
They're nature's greatest joke, and making men
She sought but to amuse the gods.

JACKAL. Forsooth I know the cause of my surprise
The day when I heard laughter from the skies.

HYÆNA. I say they know it, and to prove my word

Let me but tell you of the news I heard.
They are ashaméd of their naked state,
And some, more wise than others, have of late
Sought leaves and vines to hide their horrid flesh.
Thus covered like the case-worms on the trees,
They seek the hardness of their fate to ease,
The very act confessing their distress.

JACKAL. Here comes a man, we'll call him to account;
Let him excuse himself as best he may.

MAN. Kind friends, have patience, for I can
Do things you cannot, since I am a man.
Erect upon my hinder legs I lose
In speed and looks perchance, but I may use
My hands in godlike manner to create.
My hands thus freed, the brain will grow,
Guiding the tool, till I shall know
To weave the pattern of my human fate.

HYÆNA. To do the work of gods is then your dream.
Oh friends! how can a creature thus blaspheme?

BIRD. To walk on one's hind legs is quite a plan:
To that extent I will defend the man.
The front legs freed may serve a useful end
When, feather-decked, as wings they upward send
Our bodies, soaring far above the earth,
Where in the air we carol forth our mirth.

MAN. Sublime it is to fly, but better yet
To conquer nature with the mind, and so to get
Her forces held and altered to our use.
The working hand and thinking head unite,

Till weakness is converted into might,
And praise succeeds abuse.
Thus may we hold the earth and even try
Though featherless and handed, yet to fly.

BIRD. The man's insane, what better proof
Than his mad words? Let's hold aloof,
And leave him to his wretched fate,
Striving alone to reach the golden gate
Of heaven, and in godlike ways
Command the earth and hold the very rays
Of sun above to serve his foolish ends.

[*The animals draw aloof.*]

MAN. [*To himself.*] They rightly call me weak, they rightly say
I am ashaméd.
This body would I hide, and in this mind
Stir doubt and fear, my very soul doth quake
With strange forebodings of a new-born sense,
The sense of sin. How can I make
My peace with earth below or heaven above?
By mental strife or fruits of conscious love
Atone for my mistake?
        ★ ★ ★ ★ ★ ★ ★ ★
The die is cast, the choice is past,
And choosing once, I stand condemned
To ever choose again. So let it be, since I am free,
My fate lies in my hands,
Frail, imperfect, fasting ever,
Stumbling on till death may sever
Chains that bind the soul:
May heaven judge me by my meaning,
Striving, searching, ever gleaning

Parts of nature's whole.

ANIMALS. [*Regarding* MAN *from distance.*] The man strides forth,
    his eyes ablaze,
He means to conquer, win the praise
Of earth and sky.
Full strange it is he has no qualms,
He shows no dread, or vague alarms,
No fear to die!

Act V

The Present Day. [*Enter* MARS, PLEBS, PAX, PRÆCEPTOR.]

MARS. Hear the sound of marching soldiers,
Cannon thunder on the height,
Clash of arms and cry of battle,
Lurid camp-fires in the night.
Onward men, and try your valor,
Now or never do your best,
Forward now and slay the foeman,
Mars will put you to the test.

PAX. Though the din of battle ringeth
Loud and fierce on either hand,
Time, the Lord's good servant bringeth
Peace throughout the land.
Shall it be the peace of living,
Herald of a better day,
Former foes in friendship giving
Each what e'er he may?
Else the peace of dire destruction,
Death, the victor now supreme,

Lost the hope of reconstruction,
Social progress but a dream.
Choose, O Plebs, while yet you may,
The falling night drives out the day.

PLEBS. No choice is mine, this awful fate
Is born upon the wings of time,
The angel host at Heaven's gate
Are partners in the crime.

PRÆCEPTOR. Good pupil, Plebs, I told it so
To thee in younger, brighter days:
In subtile ways I made thee know
A path of logic through the maze
Of thought and action, hate and fear:
I taught, and teaching, bade thee hear.

PAX. Taught him to think the devil's hand
Must ever rule throughout the land!

PRÆCEPTOR. Kind peace, I bid him love thy name,
To hate the devil and his kind,
To feel the horror and the shame
That burdens all mankind.
I told him this, but bid him know
The ages could not change,
The future from the past must flow.
He must not think it strange
If Mars in might should stalk abroad,
And Pax lay vanquished by the sword.
So must he stand to guard his own,
Be guided by the past alone.

PAX. Be guided by the past, indeed!

Then know the past, its teachings clear,
To him who hath the head to read
And heart to banish fear.
The teaching of the past is this,
That day contrasts with night,
That custom's slaves must ever miss
The path upon the height.
The child condemned on every side
Grows up to be the future's bride.

Thomas Hardy

In a Museum

Striking prehistoric imagery recurs in the work of English novelist and poet THOMAS HARDY (1840-1928), *from Henry Knight's strange encounter with a trilobite fossil in* A Pair of Blue Eyes (1873) *to the pseudo-Carboniferous scenery of* The Return of the Native (1878).[1] *Indeed, issues of survival, extinction, evolution, and natural or sexual selection are rarely far from his writing. This short poem was inspired by a cast of the beautifully intricate fossil skeleton of* Archaeopteryx, *an evolutionary link between birds and dinosaurs. Hardy, who observed this cast at the Royal Albert Memorial Museum, Exeter, in 1915, published the poem two years later, in the collection* Moments of Vision and Miscellaneous Verses.

I

HERE's the mould of a musical bird long passed from light,
Which over the earth before man came was winging;
There's a contralto voice I heard last night,
That lodges in me still with its sweet singing.

II

Such a dream is Time that the coo of this ancient bird
Has perished not, but is blent, or will be blending
Mid visionless wilds of space with the voice that I heard,
In the full-fugued song of the universe unending.

1 Patricia Ingham, "Hardy and *The Wonders of Geology*," *Review of English Studies*, 31 (1980), 59-64.

Clotilde Graves as Richard Dehan

The Great Beast of Kafue

This somber tale was written by the Anglo-Irish novelist and playwright
Clotilde Graves *(1863-1932), much of whose work, including this
story, was published under the name Richard Dehan.*[1] *It appeared in*
Under the Hermés *(1917), one of Graves's many short story collections. The story is set after the Second Anglo-Boer War of 1899-1902,
Kafue being in what is now Zambia. At first, the titular "Great Beast"
appears to face the same fate as those other prehistoric animals rediscovered
by trigger-happy short story protagonists, but the action takes a surpris-
ing turn. Graves's conceit that a giant sauropod dinosaur might survive
in what were then the British protectorates of Rhodesia was likely based
on a rumor spread by the animal merchant Carl Hagenbeck in his book*
Beasts and Men *(1909).*[2]

It happened at our homestead on the border of South-eastern
Rhodesia, seventy miles from Tuli Concession, some three
years after the War.

A September storm raged, the green, broad-leaved tobacco-
plants tossed like the waves of the ocean I had crossed and
re-crossed, journeying to and coming back from my dead
mother's wet, sad country of Ireland to this land of my father
and his father's father.

1 Jenny Bloodworth, "Clotilde Graves: Journalist, Dramatist and Novelist.
Writing to Survive in the Late Nineteenth and Early Twentieth Century,"
unpublished Ph.D. thesis, University of Leicester, 2013.
2 Daniel Loxton and Donald R. Prothero, *Abominable Science!: Origins of
the Yeti, Nessie, and Other Famous Cryptids* (New York: Columbia University
Press, 2013), 270-271.

The acacias and kameel thorns and the huge cactus-like euphorbia that fringed the water-courses and the irrigation channels had wrung their hands all day without ceasing, like Makalaka women at a native funeral. Night closed in: the wooden shutters were barred, the small-paned windows fastened, yet they shook and rattled as though human beings without were trying to force a way in. Whitewash fell in scales from the big tie-beams and cross-rafters of the farm kitchen, and lay in little powdery drifts of whiteness on the solid table of brown locust-tree wood, and my father's Dutch Bible that lay open there. Upon my father's great black head that was bent over the Book, were many streaks and patches of white that might not be shaken or brushed away.

It had fallen at the beginning of the War, that snow of sorrow streaking the heavy curling locks of coarse black hair. My pretty young mother—an Irishwoman of the North, had been killed in the Women's Laager at Gueldersdorp during the Siege. My father served as Staats gunner during the Investment—and now you know the dreadful doubt that heaped upon those mighty shoulders a bending load, and sprinkled the black hair with white.

You are to see me in my blue drill roundabout and little homespun breeches sitting on a cricket in the shadow of the table-ledge, over against the grim *sterk* figure in the big, thong-seated armchair.

There would be no going to bed that night. The dam was over-full already, and the next spate from the hill sluits might crack the great wall of mud-cemented saw-squared boulders, or overflow it, and lick away the work of years. The farm-house roof had been rebuilt since the shell from the English naval gun had wrecked it, but the work of men to-day is not like that of the men of old. My father shook his head, contemplating the new masonry, and the whitewash fell as though in confirmation of his expressed doubts.

I had begged to stay up rather than lie alone in the big bed in my father's room. Nodding with sleepiness I should have denied, I carved with my two-bladed American knife at a little canoe I meant to swim in the shallower river-pools. And as I shaped the prow I dreamed of something I had heard on the previous night.

A traveller of the better middle-class, overseer of a coal-mine working "up Buluwayo" way, who had stayed with us the previous night and gone on to Tuli that morning, had told the story. What he had failed to tell I had haltingly spelled out of the three-weeks-old English newspaper he had left behind.

So I wrought, and remembered, and my little canoe swelled and grew in my hands. I was carrying it on my back through a forest of tall reeds and high grasses, forcing a painful way between the tough wrist-thick stems, with the salt sweat running down into my eyes. . . . Then I was in the canoe, wielding the single paddle, working my frail crank craft through sluggish pools of black water, overgrown with broad spiny leaves of water-plants cradling flowers of marvellous hue. In the canoe bows leaned my grandfather's elephant-gun, the inlaid, browned-steel-barrelled weapon with the diamond-patterned stock and breech, that had always seemed to my childish eyes the most utterly desirable, absolutely magnificent possession a grown-up man might call his own.

A *paauw* made a great commotion getting up against the reeds; but does a hunter go after *paauw* with his grandfather's elephant-gun? Duck were feeding in the open spaces of sluggish black water. I heard what seemed to be the plop! of a jumping fish, on the other side of a twenty-foot high barrier of reeds and grasses. I looked up then, and saw, glaring down upon me from inconceivable heights of sheer horror, the Thing of which I had heard and read.

*   *   *   *   *

At this juncture I dropped the little canoe and clutched my father round the leg.

"What is it, *mijn jongen?*"

He, too, seemed to rouse out of a waking dream. You are to see the wide, burnt-out-looking grey eyes that were staring sorrowfully out of their shadowy caves under the shaggy eyebrows, lighten out of their deep abstraction and drop to the level of my childish face.

★　★　★　★　★

"You were thinking of the great beast of Kafue Valley, and you want to ask me if I will lend you my father's elephant-rifle when you are big enough to carry it that you may go and hunt for the beast and kill it; is that so?"

My father grasped his great black beard in one huge knotted brown hand, and made a rope of it, as was his way. He looked from my chubby face to the old-fashioned black-powder 8-bore that hung upon the wall against a leopard kaross, and back again, and something like a smile curved the grim mouth under the shaggy black and white moustache.

"The gun you shall have, boy, when you are of age to use it, or a 450-Mannlicher or a 600-Mauser, the best that may be bought north of the Transvaal, to shoot explosive or conical bullets from cordite cartridges. But not unless you give me your promise never to kill that beast, shall money of mine go to the buying of such a gun for you. Come now, let me have your word!"

Even to my childish vanity the notion of my solemnly entering into a compact binding my hand against the slaying of the semi-fabulous beast-marvel of the Upper Rhodesian swamps, smacked of the fantastic if not of the absurd. But my father's eyes had no twinkle in them, and I faltered out the promise they commanded.

"*Nooit—nooit* will I kill that beast! It should kill me, rather!"

"Your mother's son will not be *valsch* to a vow. For so would you, son of my body, make of me, your father, a traitor to an oath that I have sworn!"

The great voice boomed in the rafters of the farm kitchen, vying with the baffled roaring of the wind that was trying to get in, as I had told myself, and lie down, folding wide quivering wings and panting still, upon the sheepskin that was spread before the hearth.

"But—but why did you swear?"

I faltered out the question, staring at the great bearded figure in homespun jacket and tan-cord breeches and *veldschoens*, and thought again that it had the hairy skin of Esau and the haunted face of Saul.

Said my father, grimly—

"Had I questioned my father so at twice your age, he would have skinned my back and I should have deserved it. But I cannot beat your mother's son, though the Lord punish me for my weakness. . . . And you have the spirit of the *jager* in you, even as I. What I saw you may one day see. What I might have killed, that shall you spare, because of me and my oath. Why did I take it upon me, do you ask? Even though I told you, how should a child understand? What is it you are saying? Did I really, really see the beast? Ay, by the Lord!" said my father thoughtfully, "I saw him. And never can a man who has seen, forget that sight. What are you saying?"

The words tumbled over one another as I stammered in my hurry—

"But—the English traveller said only one white man besides the Mashona hunter has seen the beast, and the newspaper says so too."

"*Natuurlijk.* And the white man is me," thundered the deep voice.

I hesitated.

"But since the planting of the tobacco you have not left the *plaats*. And the newspaper is of only three weeks back."

"*Dat spreekt*, but the story is older than that, *mijn jongen*. It is the third time it has been dished up in the *Buluwayo Courant* sauced up with lies to change the taste as belly-lovers have their meat. But I am the man who saw the beast of Kafue, and the story that is told is my story, nevertheless!"

I felt my cheeks beginning to burn. Wonderful as were the things I knew to be true of the man, my father, this promised to be the most wonderful of all.

"It was when I was hunting in the Zambezi Country," said my father, "three months after the *Commandaants* of the Forces of the United Republics met at Klerksdorp to arrange conditions of peace——"

"With the English generals," I put in.

"With the English, as I have said. You had been sent to your—to *her* people in Ireland. I had not then thought of rebuilding the farm. For more than a house of stones had been thrown down for me, and more than so many thousand acres of land laid waste . . .

"Where did I go? *Ik wiet niet.* I wondered *op en neer* like the evil spirit in the Scriptures," the great corded hand shut the Book and reached over and snuffed the tallow-dip that hung over at the top, smoking and smelling, and pitched the black wick-end angrily on the red hearth-embers. "I sought rest and found none, either for the sole of my foot or the soul in my body. There is bitterness in my mouth as though I have eaten the spotted lily-root of the swamps. I cannot taste the food I swallow, and when I lie down at night something lies down with me, and when I rise up, it rises too and goes by my side all day."

I clung to the leg of the table, not daring to clutch my father's. For his eyes did not seem to see me any more, and a blob of foam quivered on his beard that hung over his great breast in a shadowy cascade dappled with patches of white. He went on, I scarcely daring to breathe—

"For, after all, do I know it is not I who killed her? That accursed day, was I not on duty as ever since the beginning of the investment, and is it not a splinter from a Maxim Norden-feld fired from an eastern gun-position, that———" Great drops stood on my father's forehead. His huge frame shook. The clenched hand resting on the solid table of locust-beam, shook that also, shaking me, clinging to the table-leg with my heart thumping violently, and a cold, crawling sensation among the roots of my curls.

"At first, I seem to remember there was a man hunting with me. He had many Kaffir servants and four Mashona hunters and wagons drawn by salted tailless spans, fine guns and costly tents, plenty of stores and medicine in little sugar-pills, in bot-tles with silver tops. But he sickened in spite of all his quinine, and the salted oxen died, just like beasts with tails; and besides, he was afraid of the Makwakwa and the Mashengwa with their slender poisoned spears of reeds. He turned back at last. I pushed on."

There was a pause. The strange, iron-grey, burnt-out eyes looked through me and beyond me, then the deep, trembling voice repeated, once more changing the past into the present tense—

"I push on west. My life is of value to none. The boy—is he not with her people? Shall I live to have him back under my roof and see in his face one day the knowledge that I have killed his mother? Nay, nay, I will push on!"

There was so long a silence after this that I ventured to move. Then my father looked at me, and spoke to me, not as though I were a child, but as if I had been another man.

"I pushed on, crossing the rivers on a blown-up goatskin and some calabashes, keeping my father's elephant-gun and my cartridges dry by holding them above my head. Food! For food there were thorny orange cucumbers with green pulp, and the native women at the kraals gave me cakes of maize and milk. I hunted and killed rhino and elephant and hippo and lion until the head-men of the Mashengwa said the beast was a god of theirs and the slaying of it would bring a pestilence upon their tribe, and so I killed no more. And one day I shot a cow hippo with her calf, and she stood to suckle the ugly little thing while her life was bleeding out of her, and after that I ceased to kill. I needed little, and there were yet the green-fleshed cucumbers, and ground-nuts, and things like those."

He made a rope of his great beard, twisting it with a rasping sound.

"Thus I reached the Upper Kafue Valley where the great grass swamps are. No railway then, running like an iron snake up from Buluwayo to bring the ore down from the silver-mines that are there.

"Six days' *trek* from the mines—I went on foot always, you will understand!—six days' journey from the mines, above where L'uengwe River is wedded to Kafue, as the Badanga say—is a big water.

"It is a lake, or rather, two lakes, not round, but shaped like the bowls of two wooden spoons. A shore of black, stone-like baked mud round them, and a bridge of the same stone is between them, so that they make the figure that is for 8."

The big, hairy forefinger of my father's right hand traced the numeral in the powdered whitewash that lay in drifts upon the table.

"That is the shape of the lakes, and the Badanga say that they have no bottom, and that fish taken from their waters remain raw and alive, even on the red-hot embers of their cooking stove. They are a lazy, dirty people who live on snakes and frogs and grubs—tortoise and fish. And they gave me to eat and told me, partly in words of my own moder Taal they had picked up somehow, partly in sign language, about the Great

Beast that lives in the double lake that is haunted by the spirits of their dead."

I waited, my heart pumping at the bottom of my throat, my blood running horribly, delightfully chill, to hear the rest.

"The hunting spirit revives in a man, even at death's door, to hear of an animal the like of which no living hunter has ever brought down. The Badanga tell me of this one, tales, tales, tales! They draw it for me with a pointed stick on a broad green leaf, or in the ashes of their cooking-fires. And I have seen many a great beast, but, *voor den donder!* never a beast such as that!"

I held on to my stool with both hands.

"I ask the Badanga to guide me to the lair of the beast for all the money I have upon me. They care not for gold, but for the old silver hunting-watch I carry they will risk offending the spirits of their dead. The old man who has drawn the creature for me, he will take me. And it is January, the time of year in which he has been before known to rise and bellow—*Maar!*—below like twenty buffalo bulls in spring-time, for his mate to rise from those bottomless deeps below and drink the air and sun."

So there are two great beasts! Neither the traveller nor the newspaper nor my father, until this moment, had hinted at that!

"The she-beast is much the smaller and has no horns. This my old man makes clear to me, drawing her with the point of his fish-spear on smooth mud. She is very sick the last time my old man has seen her. Her great moon-eyes are dim, and the stinking spume dribbles from her jaws. She can only float in the trough of the wave that her mate makes with his wallowings, her long scaly neck lying like a dead python on the oily black water. My old man thinks she was then near death. I ask him how long ago that is? Twenty times have the blue lake-lilies blossomed, the lilies with the sweet seeds that the Badanga make bread of—since. And the great bull has twice been heard bellowing, but never has he been seen of man since then."

My father folded his great arms upon the black-and-white cascade of beard that swept down over his shirt of homespun and went on—

"Twenty years. Perhaps, think I, my old man has lied to me! But we are at the end of the last day's journey. The sun has set and night has come. My old man makes me signs we are near the lakes and I climb a high mahogo, holding by the limbs of the wild fig that is hugging the tree to death."

My father spat into the heart of the glowing wood ashes, and said—

"I see the twin lakes lying in the midst of the high grass-swamps, barely a mile away. The black, shining waters cradle the new moon of January in their bosom, and the blue star that hangs beneath her horn, and there is no ripple on the surface, or sign of a beast, big or little. And I despise myself, I, the son of honest Booren, who have been duped by the lies of a black man-ape. I am coming down the tree, when through the night comes a long, hollow booming, bellowing roar that is not the cry of any beast I know. Thrice it comes, and my old man of the Badanga, squatting among the roots of the mahogo, nods his wrinkled bald skull, and says, squinting at me, 'Now you have heard, Baas, will you go back or go on?'

"I answer, '*Al recht uit!*'

"For something of the hunting spirit has wakened in me. And I see to the cleaning of the elephant-gun and load it carefully before I sleep that night."

I would have liked to ask a question but the words stuck in my throat.

"By dawn of day we have reached the lakes," went on my father. "The high grass and the tall reeds march out into the black water as far as they may, then the black stone beach shelves off into depths unknown.

"He who has written up the story for the Buluwayo news-paper says that the lake was once a volcano and that the crumbly black stone is lava. It may be so. But volcanoes are holes in the tops of mountains, while the lakes lie in a valley-bottom, and he who wrote cannot have been there, or he would know there are two, and not one.

"All the next night we, camping on the belt of stony shore that divides lake from lake, heard nothing. We ate the parched grain and baked grubs that my old man carried in a little bag. We lighted no fire because of the spirits of the dead Badanga that would come crowding about it to warm themselves, and poison us with their breath. My old man said so, and I humoured him. My dead needed no fire to bring her to me. She was there always . . .

"All the day and the night through we heard and saw noth-ing. But at windstill dawn of the next day I saw a great curving ripple cross the upper lake that may be a mile and a half wide; and the reeds upon the nearer shore were wetted to the knees as by the wave that is left in the wake of a steamer, and oily patches of scum, each as big as a barn floor, befouled the calm water, and there was a cold, strange smell upon the next breeze, but nothing more.

"Until at sunset of the next day, when I stood upon the mid-most belt of shore between lake and lake, with my back to the blood-red wonder of the west and my eyes sheltered by my hand as I looked out to where I had seen the waters divided as a man furrows earth with the ploughshare, and felt a shadow fall over me from behind, and turned . . . and saw . . . *Alamachtig!*"

I could not breathe. At last, at last, it was coming!

"I am no coward," said my father, in his deep resounding bass, "but that was a sight of terror. My old man of the Badanga had bolted like a rock-rabbit. I could hear the dry reeds crashing as he broke through. And the horned head of the beast, that was as big as a wagon-trunk shaking about on the top of a python-neck that topped the tallest of the teak-trees or mahogos that grow in the grass-swamps, seemed as if it were looking for the little human creature that was trying to run away.

"*Voor den donder!* how the water rises up in columns of smoke-spray as the great beast lashes it with his crocodile-tail! His head is crocodile also, with horns of rhino, his body has the bulk of six hippo bulls together. He is covered with armour of scales, yellow-white as the scales of leprosy, he has paddles like a tortoise. God of my fathers, what a beast to see! I forget the gun I hold against my hip—I can only stand and look, while the cold, thick puffs of stinking musk are brought to my nostrils and my ear-drums are well-nigh split with the bellowing of the beast. Ay! and the wave of his wallowings that wets one to the neck is foul with clammy ooze and oily scum.

"Why did the thing not see me? I did not try to hide from those scaly-lidded great eyes, yellow with half-moon-shaped pupils, I stood like an idol of stone. Perhaps that saved me, or I was too little a thing to vent a wrath so great upon. He Who in the beginning made herds of beasts like that to move upon the face of the waters, and let this one live to show the pigmy world of to-day what creatures were of old, knows. I do not. I was dazed with the noise of its roarings and the thundering blows of its huge tail upon the water; I was drenched with the spume of its snortings and sickened with the stench it gave forth. But I never took my eyes from it, as it spent its fury, and little by little I came to understand.

"*Het is jammer* to see anything suffer as that beast was suffering. Another man in my place would have thought as much, and when it lay still at last on the frothing black water, a bullet from the elephant-rifle would have lodged in the little stupid brain behind the great moon-eye, and there would have been an end . . .

"But I did not shoot!"

★   ★   ★   ★   ★   ★

It seemed an age before my father spoke again, though the cuckoo-clock had only ticked eight times.

"No! I would not shoot and spare the beast, dinosaurus or brontosaurus, or whatever the wiseacres who have not seen him may name him, the anguish that none had spared me. '*Let him go on!*' said I. '*Let him go on seeking her in the abysses that no lead-line may ever fathom, without consolation, without hope! Let him rise to the sun and the breeze of spring through miles of the cold black water, and find her not, year after year until the ending of the world. Let him call her through the mateless nights until Day and Night rush together at the sound of the Trumpet of the Judgment, and Time shall be no more!*'"

Crash!

The great hand came down upon the solid locust-wood table, breaking the spell that had bound my tongue.

"I—do not understand," I heard my own child-voice saying. "Why was the Great Beast so sorry? What was he looking for?"

"His mate who died. Ay, at the lower end of the second lake, where the water shallows, her bones were sticking up like the bleached timbers of a wrecked ship. And He and She being the last of their kind upon the earth, therefore he knows desolation ... and shall know it till death brings forgetfulness and rest. Boy, the wind is fallen, the rain has spent itself, it is time that you go to bed."

CPSIA information can be obtained
at www.ICGtesting.com
Printed in the USA
LVHW090939100421
683894LV00033B/389

9 781948 405744